SECOND CHANCE
SUMMER

SECOND CHANCE SUMMER

SARAH KAPIT

HENRY HOLT AND COMPANY

NEW YORK

Henry Holt and Company, *Publishers since 1866*
Henry Holt® is a registered trademark of Macmillan Publishing Group, LLC
120 Broadway, New York, NY 10271 • mackids.com

Our books may be purchased in bulk for promotional, educational, or
business use. Please contact your local bookseller or the Macmillan Corporate
and Premium Sales Department at (800) 221-7945 ext. 5442 or by email at
MacmillanSpecialMarkets@macmillan.com.

Library of Congress Cataloging-in-Publication Data

Names: Kapit, Sarah, author.
Title: Second chance summer / Sarah Kapit.
Description: First edition. | New York : Henry Holt Books and Company,
2023. | Audience: Ages 8–12. | Audience: Grades 4–6. | Summary:
When twelve-year-old former best friends Maddie and Chloe arrive at
camp and discover they are cabin mates, they must decide if they want
to continue staying mad at each other or give their friendship another go.
Identifiers: LCCN 2022047058 | ISBN 9781250860903 (hardback)
Subjects: CYAC: Camps—Fiction. | Best friends—Fiction. |
Friendship—Fiction.
Classification: LCC PZ7.1.K32 Se 2023 | DDC [Fic]—dc23
LC record available at https://lccn.loc.gov/2022047058

First edition, 2023
Book design by Mallory Grigg
Printed in the United States of America by Lakeside Book Company,
Harrisonburg, Virginia

ISBN 978-1-250-86090-3
1 3 5 7 9 10 8 6 4 2

To my sister Emily,
who always has a song

CHAPTER ONE

Maddie

NOW: JULY

I've seen the movies. I know that girls like me never get to be the star. At best, the awkward fat girl plays the sidekick. She gets a funny line or two before fading into the background.

Even so, I like to imagine my life as a film. In my head, I decide on the music, the lighting, the set. I figure out exactly where the camera ought to be positioned and when I will enter the frame.

Of course, if life really followed the Movie Rules, it would have more cinematic scenery. I most certainly would not be stuck in the back of my moms' car for three straight hours, with only the whooshing of the air conditioner as my soundtrack.

It isn't great.

"We're almost at camp, kid," Sandra tells me.

Note to the director: Sandra is one of my moms. She's pretty cool, for a mom.

"I can't wait," I say. That is only sort of a lie.

I try to keep my voice steady, even though this is the day I've been awaiting for months and months. My first day at Camp Rosewood, the only sleepaway camp in Southern California with a screenwriting program.

The very thought makes my legs jittery.

My other mom starts talking, a long and winding mono-
logue about how much she'll miss me. It soon veers into a
lecture on the importance of sunscreen. But I can't give her
my full attention, not now.

In my whole entire life—almost thirteen years—I have
never been away from home for more than a week. And even
that was just visiting Grandma and Grandpa in Florida. This
time, I'll be all on my own. The very idea is terrifying.

But a good movie hero always leaves home behind to
embark on the big adventure. Frodo, Captain Marvel, and
now me. I certainly cannot—I will not—let my nerves get
in the way.

Besides, I need to escape Pasadena. If I had the choice,
I would transfer to a new school entirely for eighth grade.
Since the moms have made it clear that isn't going to hap-
pen, I'll take a month away from home, away from everyone
I know.

I lean back in my seat. If I were in a movie, now would be
the perfect time for a Moment of Introspection—you know,
one of those scenes where the main character gazes out
the window with a deep, thoughtful frown. I try to imagine
myself at camp. One by one, the scenes unfold in my mind.
They're a little fuzzy around the edges at first, but gradually
the images sharpen. I see myself reclining by the lakeside as I
scribble brilliant words in my notebook. I see my screenwriting teacher beam at me while I share my work with the rest
of the group. I see myself onstage, ready to begin a performance. My costume fits perfectly, and I know exactly what I
need to do. The main lights dim, and then I—

What? No, that scene isn't right at all. I'm a screenwriter, not a performer. I won't be performing a single thing at Camp Rosewood.

After all, literally everyone in the whole world knows what happened the last time I was stupid enough to perform onstage. I most certainly will not be repeating that experience. Not this summer, not ever.

No, I am going to Camp Rosewood so I can learn screenwriting. Screenwriting is safe. I am good at it. And maybe—hopefully—I will make a new friend at camp. That all seems very reasonable and doable. Even if my last friend abandoned me right when I needed her the most.

But I refuse to think about *her*.

"Maddie?" Mom says. She has a habit of interrupting me when I'm in a Moment of Introspection. "You've been awfully quiet. Still there, hon?"

Blinking, I try to banish all thoughts of my ex–best friend from my mind. I cross my arms over my chest. "No, actually, I've been abducted by aliens who are invading Earth. They took the real me up to their spaceship and replaced me with a robot."

I once wrote a screenplay that was sort of like that. It was not, sadly, particularly good, but I do like the concept.

"So, you are still there. Got it," Mom says.

As the car winds through yet another barely there dirt road, I realize that people at camp won't know who I am. To them, I won't be weird Maddie Simmons. The girl who ruined the school musical. The girl who went viral for all the wrong reasons. The girl who used to be friends with Chloe

Winters. At Camp Rosewood, I can write a new script and leave last year's humiliations behind.

I will not do anything to ruin my big chance. I will not.

A large wooden sign appears, as if to punctuate my big realization. WELCOME TO CAMP ROSEWOOD, it tells me.

I chew on the edges of my lip and try to banish all of the worries and what-ifs that threaten to invade my mind. Exit bad thoughts.

Begin scene.

By the time we reach Cabin 7B, the cabin where I will be spending the next four weeks, my arm muscles ache and the rest of me is gross and sweaty. Still, this is a big moment, the kind of moment that sets the scene for the whole movie. I take in the setting—a dusty path winding up to a row of cabins nestled in thick trees.

Cabin 7B itself is definitely not a film set. It's too small and too wooden, with nothing much of visual interest. Well, I guess I won't be spending a lot of time here anyway. Camp Rosewood must have loads of better locations, places where I can curl up with my notebook and the movies in my mind.

For now, I sigh and consider how best to haul my trunk up the stairs. Just as I start lifting it off the ground, Sandra sprints over and grabs one of the handles. "You don't need a sprained ankle on your first day of camp."

She's just teasing me, but I blush anyway. I have sprained my ankle no fewer than three times over the last four years. Every single one of these incidents occurred because of something horrendously embarrassing. Most recently, I

tripped over the grass while running to greet my dog, Hulk. That little misstep put me in an ankle brace for three weeks.

I have something called dyspraxia. It's a disability, and basically a medical-ish way of saying that I'm really clumsy. Mom and Sandra say that it doesn't make me less than anyone else—it's just that my brain works differently. Still, having a brain that works differently can be really, really annoying.

As recent events have shown.

So even though I would like to lift the trunk myself, Sandra is probably right. I don't need to start camp with an injury. I accept her help and we start to haul the weighty trunk up the stairs together.

"Almost there, kid," Sandra says.

She leans forward to push the door open, but someone else opens it for us. A tall, thin white woman with auburn hair and big sunglasses. I know this woman, somehow, but my brain refuses to put all of the pieces together. She can't be who I think she is. Because that would mean catastrophe.

"Maddie!" she says. "How wonderful. I haven't seen you in a while."

I stare at her, too shocked to say a single word. Sandra glares at me, and I'm pretty sure she wants to scold me about my lack of manners. Fortunately, the woman who greeted me has a habit of talking through any and all moments of silence. Today is no exception.

"Chloe didn't mention that you would be here!" she exclaims.

The familiar name snaps me out of my shock. "Chloe?"

And then, looking past the woman, I see *her*—brilliant red hair, fashionably thin frame, and a pimple-free face that most definitely is not smiling. My former best friend, Chloe Winters.

"Hi, Maddie," she mumbles.

CHAPTER TWO

Chloe

This is so not part of the plan.

For a long moment, I don't say anything. Neither does Maddie. I guess we don't know what to say. Or at least I don't. After minute five bazillion, I have no choice but to break the silence.

"I'm over there," I say. I point to the bunk I picked.

Maddie's eyes narrow, and she nods. "Okay," she says.

That's it. *Okay*.

I didn't exactly expect a hug or whatever. But the shortness of her response still stings. Once, Maddie and I would have had plenty to say to each other. Once, we would have picked out bunks right next to each other so we could talk and whisper at night.

Not now. Now she only wants to know what bunk I'm in so she can avoid it. And the worst part is that it kind of is mostly my fault.

I try not to watch Maddie as she and her moms drag her trunk to the opposite end of the cabin. But I do. She picks a bed by the wall. That's as far away from me as she can get without setting up camp in the bathroom or something. (At least she didn't do that?)

Shaking myself, I return to my own bunk.

Since I have the worst luck ever, I still can't get away from conversations I do not want to have. Cordelia has seen to it. (I call my mother Cordelia, not Mom and definitely not Mommy. I think being called Mom makes her feel old.)

"This is all rather rustic, isn't it?" Cordelia says, in that way of hers that isn't really asking a question at all. "Are you sure you'll be okay, Chlo? I know how you are about your beauty sleep."

I grind my teeth. Okay, yeah. Usually I'm not a hiking and campfire kind of girl. More of a glitter bath bomb and pedicure girl, really. But seriously. I'd sleep in a cave full of spider eggs in exchange for a month free of my mother. A month where I don't have to be Chloe Winters, former television star. Even if I do have to share a cabin with someone who hates me.

But I don't say any of this. Obviously. Instead, I put on a fake smile for Cordelia. The patented Chloe Winters smile I use for all my auditions and interviews. "I'll be fine. I think it will be good to . . . you know, try something different."

"Hmmph."

I can't tell what *hmmph* is supposed to mean, but I can only assume that Cordelia will make her opinion known sooner or later. Probably sooner.

"If you think you can handle rough living, dear, then have at it." She glances around the room and lowers her voice noticeably. "I didn't realize you and Maddie were still on the outs."

I shrug. As if I don't care at all. Maybe if I keep pretending, it will become true. Luckily, I'm a really good actor.

"Lynn was the one who told me about Camp Rose-wood," Cordelia says. "I suppose I forgot to tell you."

Lynn is one of Maddie's moms. She and Cordelia are friends, in that weird way moms are friends with other moms. That used to be a good thing. Now? Not so much.

"I'll be fine," I say again.

Cordelia smiles brightly at me.

"I know you will, darling. And I'll be just a phone call away."

Like that's such a great thing. I nod anyway. Cordelia, of course, continues talking at full speed. I tune her out until I hear one of my least favorite phrases.

"I really do think your career is going to take off soon," Cordelia says.

I give another grunt. I'm an actor. Or at least I was. Over the past year, I've gone on a million auditions and gotten a million rejections. In fact, the recent highlight of my acting career was a commercial. The world's most embarrassing commercial, in fact. If the auditions that come my way are anything like that, I'll take a hard pass.

Cordelia says all the rejections are just how Hollywood works, and that's true. But also, it's my age. I'm twelve and I pretty much look twelve. Too young for teenage parts but too old for kid parts. Cordelia has yet to recognize this basic fact.

After several more minutes of babble, Cordelia pats me on the back. "I know you'll be fine, dear," she tells me before she sweeps away from the cabin. "Love you."

9

It's wrong, but as I watch her leave, a slow smile creeps across my face. Okay, so maybe Maddie being here isn't ideal. Definitely not. But with my mother gone . . . maybe I don't have to be Chloe Winters, Child Actor, for the next month. Maybe I can just be Chloe.

Whoever she is.

Finally, Cordelia is out of sight. Thanks, universe!

I should go around and introduce myself to everyone. But . . . well, between Maddie and Cordelia and unpacking my stuff, I'm tired. I don't feel like meeting new people. So I slide my headphones on and start listening to the soundtrack for *Wicked*, a.k.a. the best musical ever. Listening to Elphaba and Galinda do their thing always takes me to a happy place, or at least a more happy place. Sure, Elphaba is green, and I guess that's rough or whatever. But at least *she* doesn't have a mom who worries about how her next haircut will impact her public image.

Halfway through "The Wizard And I," someone interrupts me. Rude.

I look at her. She's a white girl with dirty blond hair, freckles, and a smile that has got to be fake.

"I'm sorry," she says, in the least-sorry voice ever. "But I just have to know. Are you Chloe Winters? From *Super Hero Kids*?"

Running a hand through my hair, I sigh. Of course. *Super Hero Kids* may be permanently canceled, but everyone still recognizes me from it.

Part of me wants to deny it. I probably would, if not for

the fact that I don't think I can keep up the act for an entire summer.

"Yeah," I tell the annoying girl. "I'm Chloe."

Her face lights up like a stage when it's time for the final dance number. "I knew it! I used to watch the show all the time. You . . . you're Miranda."

"No, I'm not," I say before I can stop myself. "Miranda is a character. She isn't real. I can't read minds and I'm not a superhero. I'm . . . I'm just Chloe."

"I know that. But I loved you!"

I bite my tongue to hold back a mean response. This girl, whoever she is, doesn't love me. She doesn't know me, and if she did, she wouldn't like me at all. Not the real me, anyway. I clench my fists, and my fingernails dig into the skin of my palms. Through it all, I give the girl a Chloe Winters Smile.

"It was very nice to meet you," I say. Even though nothing about it had been nice, Cordelia has trained me on how to deal with annoying fans.

The girl beams. Again.

"Abso-freaking-lutely! We're going to be friends, I hope. My name is Mara, by the way. I'm an actor. Well, I hope to be an actor. I'm not like you. I've been to a few open call auditions, but they didn't work out."

Well, yeah, probably because you irritated the casting director so much.

"I personally think that anyone who acts is an actor," I say. A total lie. Lies are useful for surviving blech-worthy conversations like this one.

"Gosh, you're just so nice! Like Miranda."

Yeah, this girl doesn't know me.

"Thank you," I say.

"My friends back home aren't going to believe me when I tell them how I met you and shared a cabin with you and everything."

All I want is to end this conversation, please and thank you. Unfortunately, that's not happening.

"Hey, so I've been wondering . . ." she says.

I manage to hold back a sigh. Really, I deserve an Oscar for this performance.

"I hope it's not rude to ask or anything, but why aren't you on TV anymore?"

Of course. Mara would be exactly the kind of person to bring up my least favorite topic ever.

My hands fidget. I barely stop myself from grimacing. "Actually, I have been on a few episodes of that crime show. And, you know, some commercials."

For some reason, I want to defend my recent career accomplishments. Even though Mara is right. I haven't done anything special since the streaming service canceled *Super Hero Kids*.

"Oh, right!" Mara says, completely oblivious to the fact that I so do not want to talk about any of this. "I saw you in that commercial for . . . what was the medication called?"

"Tortasil Relief," I mumble, staring at the wooden floor planks.

The very mention of *that* commercial makes flames erupt on my face. My cheeks match my hair, probably.

If my career in general is my least favorite topic, then this is my least-least favorite topic. I mean, isn't it bad enough that my latest acting work is starring in a commercial for menstrual cramp medicine made for preteens? Does everyone really have to remind me of that fact every five minutes for the rest of my life?

"Oh, yeah. Well, you were great!" Mara says.

Now I know she's just sucking up. My performance mostly involved a lot of whining about cramps. Which, to be fair, did require a ton of acting. I haven't had my period yet for real.

I search for a nice-but-boring response to Mara's compliment. Nothing comes to me.

But I'm saved. Audrey, the counselor who greeted me earlier, enters the main cabin once again. Only she's not wearing jean shorts and a Camp Rosewood T-shirt anymore. Instead, Audrey looks like a character out of an old movie, in a vintage white dress and wide-brimmed hat covered in pink roses. She probably can't even walk through most doors without squishing the hat, but it doesn't matter. This is a costume for the stage.

I know who she is immediately, of course: Eliza Doolittle from *My Fair Lady*.

My skin tingles. Audrey must be a musical theater person. I wonder if she's in charge of the camp musical. I've read the Camp Rosewood website three million times. There's a dramatic play—probably some seriously boring stuff written by a dead white man about other dead white men. That's what Maddie would say. But the camp also puts on a musical.

I want to do the musical. Cordelia wants me to do the play, because of course she does. I sort of assumed I'd be doing what she wants me to do. But I want what I want.

Because she has zero manners, Mara interrupts my thought. "I don't get it," she says. "What's with the costume? Who is she supposed to be?"

"Eliza Doolittle," I tell her. "Made famous by Audrey Hepburn in 1964." This time, I can't keep the edge out of my voice. Really, *My Fair Lady* is a classic.

"Who's that?"

I don't answer. I'm not paying attention to Annoying Mara. My eyes are on Audrey.

She sets down one of those old boom box things on the floor and cranks up the volume. "Wouldn't It Be Loverly" blares out—the original Broadway cast album, if I'm not wrong. (And I'm not.)

Audrey starts to dance. It's not a choreographed number so much as spinning in place, arms flailing every which way. Surrounded by the blah-ness of Cabin 7B, she doesn't exactly look like the real Eliza, out to conquer London society. But she's having a blast.

For a moment, all talk stops. Everyone stares at Audrey like, "Uh, are you supposed to be in charge or something?"

Still, this is drama camp. By the time the second chorus kicks in, a few girls have joined Audrey. One of them catches my eye—a pretty, dark-haired Latina girl who twirls with so much vigor that I feel a bit dizzy just watching her. I can't hear what she's saying, but I can see her wide smile. There isn't the slightest bit of fakeness about it.

I want to join her and Audrey. I want to twirl and spin and sing the words out loud. *Oh, wouldn't it be loverly?*

I don't.

I can't.

After all, I'm not just anyone. I'm Chloe Winters. And people are watching me.

"Pretty weird, right?"

Mara snaps me out of my . . . whatever it was. Like I really want to continue our conversation.

"What's weird?" I ask.

She waves at the dancers and makes a not-attractive face. "They look silly, don't you think? I mean, this isn't dance class."

I don't think they look silly. Okay, so maybe they do, but in a good way. I shrug and give a tight smile. Hopefully Mara will finally get the message that I am capital-*D* Done with her. For now, the next month, and until the sun swallows up the Earth.

As always, a voice that sounds like Cordelia nags at me. "An actor should show appreciation for her fans."

But really, even Cordelia might make an exception for this girl.

"Excuse me," I say finally. I use my in-charge voice. "I have to go fix my hair before dinner."

I can't think of a better excuse, but okay, whatever. That should be good enough.

"Of course! Just . . . can I ask you for one tiny favor?"

"Sure," I say. A sigh very nearly escapes me.

"Can you sign an autograph for me? Like, later?"

"Of course," I say, flashing one last fake smile.

Finally, she goes away. I feel like doing a dance of my own, but don't.

Are all the Camp Rosewood kids going to be like this?

Before I even realize what I'm doing, I turn toward my ex–best friend. Maddie is sitting on her bed, staring at some book.

Ignoring me.

Maddie

I wait for Chloe. Sometimes I feel like I spend half my life waiting for Chloe. She is the star of the show, and I am just the screenwriter. Everyone knows that while screenwriters create the script, writing and rewriting every word until everything is almost perfect, there is no movie until the star shows up.

Chloe is the kind of girl movies were made for. Me? Well, I've never seen a movie starring a chubby Jewish girl with thick glasses and a tendency to fall over at the worst possible moments. I'm the sidekick.

So I wait for Chloe.

She is worth waiting for, I remind myself. Besides, without her my big Friday night plans are taking Hulk to the backyard so he can do his business. Even thinking about it makes me feel pathetic.

Sometimes Chloe frustrates me. Maybe even a lot of the time, if I'm being completely honest. But I can't imagine a world where Chloe isn't my friend. Still, I have just about had enough of waiting. I grab my phone and start typing a message: **Are you coming?**

Just as I get ready to hit send, the doorbell rings. I jump up from the couch, hardly daring to hope. Is it Chloe?

It is. She carries a small overnight bag and smiles at me.

"I thought maybe you weren't coming," I say. Immediately, I regret my choice of words. I should be happy that

Chloe is here now, not scolding her for being late. (Even if she did keep me waiting for nearly an entire hour.)

Chloe gives me a slight shrug. "I always come, Mads. You know that."

I allow myself to relax. Although I want to know what held her up, I do not ask. I don't want Chloe to think I'm mad at her or anything like that.

Soon we're nestled in our usual positions in the den, preparing for movie night. I grab a handful of the special popcorn Mom made for us. I try not to care about the fact that the kernels feel stale in my mouth. It's still delicious, truly.

When I reach over for my cup of lemonade to wash down the popcorn, I knock it over by accident. My hands are now covered in sticky gunk. Sighing, I grab some paper towels.

Chloe barely registers the spill. I guess she's just used to my little accidents. She kicks off her shoes and settles into a ball on the couch—her favorite movie-watching position. "Your turn to pick the movie," she says.

Grinning widely, I nod. Of course, I already know it's my turn. I have a movie picked out and everything. The thing is, sometimes Chloe forgets when it's my turn to choose. Since I don't like telling her she's wrong, this means I end up watching a lot of movies Chloe likes—musicals, mostly. I like musicals, too, so I don't mind. Still, I wish Chloe would get better at remembering.

I grip the remote and start scrolling through menus. Finally, I reach my selection: *Captain Marvel*.

"Another superhero movie?" Chloe says. But she's smiling, so I know she's not too upset.

"After you made me watch that movie with all the dancing, you should be glad I've selected such a classic," I say.

"*Bye Bye Birdie* is a classic!"

"Maybe, but this one has much better special effects. Plus, women who actually do things."

"Fine, fine," Chloe says. She reaches for the popcorn.

And so we are transported into a world of superheroes and aliens, where the hero always wins. After all the uncertainty of the real world, the familiar rhythm of the movie feels like an old friend. A friend that I can count on.

Even though I've seen the movie at least five times before, I'm still on the edge of my seat during the most exciting parts. I steal a glance at Chloe every now and then, and she's transfixed, too. I give myself a figurative pat on the back for my successful movie pick.

Ever since we started seventh grade last week, fears have gnawed at me. Fears about Chloe. She hasn't said anything, exactly, but everything is different this year. For the last few years, Chloe only went to school in person part-time because she was busy filming *Super Hero Kids*. Now that the show is over, she's back at school full-time, and there are plenty of other kids who want to be her friend. She's nice to all of them, or at least fake nice. With Chloe it can be hard to tell the difference sometimes.

I know, I just *know*, that it's only a matter of time before she decides that one of them is cooler than me. Who isn't cooler than me? Once she finally realizes that, it will all be over. Maybe she won't ever actually say it, but it will happen just the same. She'll eat with other kids at lunch and partner

with them for group projects. Our sleepovers will be firmly in the past.

But for now, I still have this. The routine we've done so many times on our sleepover nights, ever since our very first one when we were eight. Back then, we watched *Frozen* for the twentieth time and sang along to all the songs.

Shifting my position slightly, I focus again on the battle between Captain Marvel and the Skrulls. Once again, everything is close to perfect.

As the closing credits roll, Chloe turns toward me. "Good pick, Mads."

"You weren't hoping for more singing and dancing?" I ask with a grin.

She smiles back. "Well, now that you mention it, I do think there was a missed opportunity for the space alien thingies to do a tap dance number."

Both of us laugh, and a warm glow fills me. "Actually," Chloe continues once we're done giggling, "I think there's some serious potential for a superhero musical. It could be your first big feature, Mads."

My first big feature. Chloe believes I can be a screenwriter, for real. Not just someone who scribbles bits of scenes into a notebook that I never show anyone besides Chloe. Obviously all of that is a long way off and everything, but still. Chloe believes in me. Although I have to say that I'm skeptical of her pitch.

"A superhero musical?" I ask. "Would the hero fly around stage and sing about saving the world? Like, 'Bad guys are

stewing. Something evil is brewing. But the world need not fear. 'Cause the best hero ever is here.'"

"Now you're getting it."

Chloe sings my own silly lyrics back at me. Of course, she makes them sound good. She belongs onstage, singing to a captivated audience.

I shake my head at her. "I think maybe the concept needs some work."

"Well, yeah," she says. "Lin-Manuel Miranda didn't write *Hamilton* in a day. But in the meantime . . . ice cream?"

She jumps up from the couch and heads toward the kitchen. This, too, is part of our routine.

I scoop cookie dough ice cream into two bowls. (Chloe's favorite flavor, of course.) For a moment, everything is exactly as it ought to be.

A few hours later, we're cocooned in our sleeping bags. I stare up at my bedroom ceiling. Once, I would have been greeted by glow-in-the-dark stars. But I tore them down at the beginning of summer because they seemed very uncool for an almost-twelve-year-old. On nights like these, I miss the stars. I wish I had something to look at besides darkness.

"Maddie?"

In the dark, Chloe's voice loses some of her usual coolness. Sort of like the cameras have been turned off. Here, I can almost imagine we're still kids who watch Disney movies and go to bed at nine thirty.

I always like our talks in the dark most of all.

"Yeah, Chlo?"

"Are you ever scared of anything?"

The question surprises me.

Because of course I am scared of things, and I don't just mean gerbils. (Although I do think they look rather suspicious and definitely not adorable like everyone else thinks.) I'm scared the other kids at school only tolerate me because of Chloe. I'm scared that I'm not actually good at writing or anything else. I'm scared that Chloe will decide she's tired of being best friends with someone so much less cool and less talented than she is.

That I am just not enough.

"Yeah," I say. "I'm scared of things."

I expect her to ask another question, but she does not. She just sighs and says, "So am I."

Maybe I should ask her what she's scared of, but I don't. I'm not sure I know how.

We lie there for several minutes more. The loudest sound in the room is the faint whoosh of Chloe's breaths, in and out and in again. I wonder if she can hear me breathe, too.

If I were with anyone besides Chloe, this moment would be unbearable in its awkwardness. But it's Chloe, so it doesn't feel awkward at all. Mostly everything just feels . . . right.

I wish I could pause this scene forever.

Chloe

I press PLAY on my phone and sink into my beanbag chair. *The Sound of Music* soundtrack fills my ears in all its glory. I hum along.

On the other side of the room, Maddie says something I can't hear. I take out my headphones. "What?" I ask. I try not to sound annoyed at the interruption.

"I said, are you done with the math homework?" Maddie asks.

"Yeah. Why?"

She stares at me. "Even problem five? I can't figure out what we're actually supposed to do."

Problem five hadn't been that difficult for me. I scoot over to Maddie's spot on the floor to help.

I try to explain math stuff, but it's hard. Maybe I'm not a good teacher. Maybe Maddie is just that bad at math. Just as we're finally about to make some progress, the door to my bedroom swings open. Uh-oh.

There is only one person in the world who barges into my room without knocking.

"Chlo!" Cordelia announces. "I have the best news."

Cordelia's definition of "best" and mine really, really are not the same. But I try to sound cool and collected in my answer.

"Yeah?"

"Darling! You've gotten a part."

Maddie being Maddie, she does her best friend duty and claps. Me? I'm not ready to start celebrating. I've auditioned for at least half a dozen parts within the last month, and there's, like, one that isn't completely horrible.

"What part?"

I'm not sure I want to know, but I have to ask.

She hesitates. And that's when I know for sure that her good news is bad, bad, bad.

"It's a commercial," she says finally. "You know how it is. Not the most glamorous job, but it will be great for your college fund."

"What part?" I repeat.

Sighing, Cordelia fixes her gaze on the wall behind my bed. Like that's so interesting. "The medication. You know, the one you auditioned for last week."

Oh no. No, no, and no.

I don't intend to say that part out loud. But apparently I do, because Maddie gives me a look of sympathy. Cordelia just gives me a Look.

"I know it's not a movie or even TV. But Chloe, this could be a gateway to so many better things!"

It can't possibly be a gateway to worse things. I don't say that, though. I still have enough sense to keep my mouth clamped shut. All I can manage is a small nod.

I glance over at Maddie. I can tell she's dying to ask about the commercial. I'm not going to explain it. At least not now, with Cordelia right here listening to my every word.

"You'll see. This is going to be great," Cordelia insists. "We start filming next week."

We. As if *we* are going to be in this commercial. I want to ask Cordelia whether she'd take my place, since this is apparently such a *great* opportunity.

I don't.

Cordelia swoops out of my room as quickly as she came in, unaware that she just ruined my life. I still can't bring myself to speak.

Maddie talks first. "So. Uh. Math. Triangles."

In that moment, I love her so much that I could burst into song. A happy one, like "Dancing Through Life." Right now, I'd love to just dance without having to worry about anything else.

We don't really talk about my mom, Maddie and me. It's not like an official rule or anything, but that's always been how we do things. Right now, talking about something else is exactly what I need. Maddie knows that. She's a good best friend that way.

I nod at her suggestion with more enthusiasm than math deserves, ever. "Right. Let's get back to triangles."

When Maddie finally completes problem five, she gives me a tentative smile. She doesn't say much—just thanks me for my help. But I can see the question she's too nice to ask.

"The commercial is for a medication," I say. "A really stupid medication."

I don't really want to talk about this. But at the same

25

time, I kind of do. Someone needs to understand my agony, and Maddie is good at listening.

"What kind of medication?" Maddie asks, because duh. That's the obvious question.

"For . . . for, you know," I say. I stare at the floor.

Maddie frowns. "Uh, sorry. You're going to have to be a little more specific, Chlo."

I sigh and start to examine my fingernails. They could use some trimming. "It's a medication for, you know. Period cramps. It's some new thing for girls our age."

"Oh!"

Maddie doesn't say anything else. For that, she has my eternal gratitude.

I should just let the subject die now. Find something else to talk about. Anything else, really.

"I didn't even want to do the audition," I say. For some reason, I just can't let this subject die. "But, you know. My mom."

Maddie knows. She nods.

"Maybe . . . maybe it won't be that bad," she says. But she doesn't sound very sure.

I snort. "Oh, I'm pretty sure it's going to be that bad."

She doesn't even try to argue.

I don't want to talk about this. I really don't. But for some reason I can't explain, I keep on talking anyway. "It's ridiculous! How am I supposed to act like I have period cramps when I've never even, you know, had my period?"

Maddie makes a noise. I'm pretty sure she's trying to

26

show sympathy. Maddie's great. The best, really. But I don't want to keep talking about this. I want to forget.

Just as she opens her mouth to speak again, I jump up from my spot on the floor.

"Anyway! It sucks. But we don't need to keep talking about things that suck. Let's get smoothies?"

I don't wait for her response before heading for the door.

Maddie follows me, of course. She always follows me.

CHAPTER THREE

Maddie

Everything is already veering off the script, and I do not like it.

I should have predicted this. I should have known Chloe would find a way to ruin my summer, stealing the lead role for herself. Because isn't that what she always does? We may be nearly two hundred miles away from Pasadena, but the patterns haven't changed. Maybe they can't change. I'm stuck in the same role as I always am. Less talented, less pretty and graceful, just *less*.

After trying and failing to read a book, I make my very best effort to talk with the other girls of Cabin 7B. I try to be, well, cool. Confident and in control. But somehow, it never quite comes together. Halfway through a conversation, my mind blanks.

Chloe's presence does not help in the least. During dinner, she sits at the next table over. Of course, she's already found new friends. I even catch her signing autographs. Truly, the whole sight makes me want to throw up my spaghetti.

I do not. Still, I can only conclude that my first few hours at Camp Rosewood have been a profound disappointment.

Soon after dinner, the counselors herd us into a different

building. Although it looks like a barn from the outside, it turns out to be a theater with a small stage. The sight of spotlights makes my stomach flutter.

I do not like spotlights.

Deep breath, Maddie. I will not have to spend any time onstage this summer. Screenwriting is an offstage activity. It is safe.

I've almost started feeling normal again when a large white woman in a red cape jumps onstage. I recognize her as the camp director.

"Hello, campers!" she says. Even without a microphone, her voice rings through the entire barn. "My name is Hannah, and I guess I'm supposed to be in charge of this place. So. Welcome to Camp Rosewood! We're going to have a fabulous month of drama, music, and all the usual camp things you know and love."

I frown. Hannah seems nice, I guess, but why didn't she talk about screenwriting?

I try to focus back on the stage as Hannah explains that tonight is open mic night. Everyone will have a chance to get up onstage and perform, if they want.

"I hope you'll share your talents with us," Hannah says. "But if you aren't comfortable getting onstage, that's cool, too."

She's talking about me. I most certainly will not be performing tonight. Or ever again, for that matter.

Kids start lining up by the stage before Hannah even finishes talking. I guess most kids here don't really need

encouragement to perform in front of an audience. This is an entire camp full of Chloes.

Part of me wants to leap up from my seat and join the rapidly growing line. That, of course, is completely ridiculous. I don't even have a talent to share.

Even so, as I watch camper after camper line up, I feel something tug at my chest.

I don't budge from my seat.

Although I definitely am not paying special attention to Chloe, I can't help but notice that she was among the first to line up, because of course.

I don't mean to stare at her, but I guess I do. The girl next to me starts to speak.

"Can you believe she's actually here at camp?" the girl says. Her voice annoys me at once, even though I know logically that it's just a voice like any other.

I force myself to remain steady when I talk. "I was a little surprised to see her," I say. Which, if anything, is an understatement. Not that this girl needs to know my whole history with Chloe.

"She's so nice! She even signed an autograph for me at dinner."

I make a noble attempt, but I cannot stop the grimace that twists across my face. The girl notices, of course.

"What?" she asks. "You don't think so?"

Well, I suppose I can't really avoid this conversation now. "No," I say. My voice only shakes a little. "I don't."

"Why not?"

She seems genuinely puzzled by this. I guess that to her,

the very idea of anyone not worshipping Chloe Winters is a matter that requires a full-on investigation.

I could give her pages worth of material on the subject. But I simply shrug and say, "I just don't like her."

The girl squints at me, as if really seeing me for the first time in this entire conversation. "You look familiar," she says. Her eyes narrow.

I clench my fists. Now I wish we could go back to talking about Chloe. That would certainly be preferable to what's about to happen.

"I . . . I don't think we know each other. Maybe I just look like someone else you know."

But the girl keeps studying my face, then finally snaps her fingers. "Right! You're the girl in that video . . . the one that went viral? During a school musical? I'm right, aren't I?"

My cheeks flush, and I wish so very much I could just walk out of here and run back to my room in Pasadena. I could stay there for the rest of my life, maybe, or at least the next six months. People will probably forget all about The Video by then, won't they?

But I am at Camp Rosewood. I can't hide out in my room. And this girl is still staring at me, clearly wanting an answer. I let out a deep sigh.

"Yeah," I say. "That was me."

"Oh, you poor thing! How terrible for you."

Although her voice drips with sympathy, something about it just feels fake to me. I frown.

"I'd really prefer not to talk about it," I say, my voice tight.

"Oh, of course!" the girl says.

Well, at least she understands that much. My shoulders lose a bit of their tension, and my breaths return to a more normal rhythm.

I should have guessed that people at camp would know about The Video. It's not the sort of thing people forget. I guess there are only so many big girls with frizzy brown hair and thick glasses in the world, so it's not like I can easily slip into anonymity. However much I wish for it. If only I were smaller and looked more like the other kids. If only the musical disaster never happened in the first place. If only I had never listened to Chloe.

The room darkens, interrupting the spiral of my thoughts. Well, at least the show is beginning.

The first performer is a boy who opens his comedy routine by making fart noises with his armpits. A few younger kids giggle, but everyone else sits and stares with blank faces. I even hear a few boos, though Hannah quickly silences them with a raised hand.

The next few acts are much better. One girl plays the flute beautifully. A boy gives a dramatic reading of Shakespeare, or at least I think it's Shakespeare. I don't fully understand all his *thees* and *thous*, but his enthusiasm shines.

Next, Chloe takes the stage. I try to keep my face still, like I don't care. Because I don't, honest to goodness.

She opens her mouth and sings. I recognize the song at once: "Defying Gravity" from *Wicked*, Chloe's favorite musical. The song has plenty of opportunities to show off—always a must for Chloe.

And show off she does. Even though I've heard Chloe sing countless times before, the power and clarity of her voice still mesmerizes me. She does not need an instrument to accompany her. Her voice is more than enough.

When she sings, I can very nearly forget about what she did, about everything that happened last spring. I can almost see her clutching a magic broomstick, ready to fly off the stage at the end of act 1. Just like the actor did when Chloe and I saw the show together at the Pantages Theatre in Hollywood.

As I watch, a familiar sensation creeps up on me. I don't want to be a real actor—I've seen how things are for kids like Chloe. Yet I still wonder. What does it feel like to stand onstage, commanding the attention of the entire room? Not because you humiliated yourself, but because you just did something spectacular. I can hardly imagine it.

Sometimes I wonder whether Chloe even appreciates what she has.

When Chloe lands the final note, everyone claps.

Even me.

CHAPTER FOUR

Chloe

I was onstage for five minutes. Six, maybe. Six minutes that could have gone on forever.

But, of course, I had to give up the stage to the next performer. That was a kid who played "Row, Row, Row Your Boat" on the guitar. Badly.

Oh well. I'll have other opportunities to perform. Other chances to soak in the feeling of ear-shattering applause.

But now I have to attend something called a "welcome campfire." It's another Camp Rosewood tradition. I don't think I'm going to like this one nearly as much as open mic night. When we reach the campfire, I hang back on the outer edges of the circle of loud, laughing people.

"You're going out for the musical, right?"

It's Audrey. She changed out of her *My Fair Lady* costume and back into a boring camp T-shirt.

"Maybe. I don't know. Maybe I'll do the play instead."

The words feel wrong in my mouth. I mean, of course I want to do the musical! I don't even care what musical it is. I want to get back that feeling I had while singing "Defying Gravity." Still, I know what Cordelia would say. She wants me to do the serious play. The one without singing and dancing and everything that makes musicals great.

So boring.

Audrey shakes her head at me. "With that voice? Come on. You have to do the musical."

I smile my most real smile and stand up just a little straighter at the compliment. I know I'm good. But hearing other people say it never fails to give me the warm fuzzies.

"I do like musicals," I say carefully. I don't commit to anything, though.

"Great! I'm in charge this year, and I can tell you that it is going to be *Hamilton*-level awesome."

Like any good musical theater kid, my attention perks up at the word *Hamilton*. I know Audrey is just trying to nudge me toward the musical. And I want it. I want it so, so much. The only problem is Cordelia's nagging voice. She may be hundreds of miles away, but that voice is still all over my head.

No, Chloe, she says. *This is not what we planned for your career. You are going to win an Oscar.*

"Chloe?" Audrey asks. "Are you okay?"

Whoops. I guess I forgot to respond out loud. I shake myself.

"Yeah," I say. "I'm okay. And . . . and I want to be in the musical."

Cordelia won't like it. I know it. Good thing she happens to be a few hundred miles away right now.

Audrey claps her hands together. "Amazing! I can't wait to get started."

The Cordelia voice in my head quiets down as I start to think about what this means. I get to spend the next month doing a musical. All day, every day. Or something close to it.

I could break out into song right now. Maybe "All That Jazz" from *Chicago*.

I don't. Obviously. That would be uncool. But I do allow myself a smile.

I turn toward Audrey. "What musical are we doing? Something classic, like *The Music Man*? I was Marian in my school's production last year." I figure that I should start campaigning for the lead role. "Or are we doing a modern show? Like *Be More Chill*? *Come From Away*, maybe?"

Audrey shakes her head, though she's still smiling. "Sorry. That's highly classified information. You'll find out at auditions tomorrow."

I deflate a little. If I knew the musical, I could better prepare for auditions. Maybe the competition here isn't exactly Broadway level, but still. I need to be prepared.

Doesn't matter, I decide. I'm good enough for the lead. Doesn't matter if it's Sarah in *Guys and Dolls* or Elsa in *Frozen*. I can do it all.

I'm about to ask Audrey more questions, but she speaks first. "Do you really want to hang out with an old crone like me?" she asks. "Go and get a marshmallow and meet some people!"

I guess that's grown-up for "go and make some friends your own age." Even though I don't really want to meet any new people, a marshmallow sounds good. I go over to the counselor who is passing out marshmallows and wooden sticks. I decide to roast four of them. (*Be careful, dear! You have to watch your waistline*, Cordelia whispers in my head. But she's not here, I remind myself. Not. Here.)

36

As I roast my marshmallows, I watch the other kids. I don't know if they were already friends or whatever, but it sure seems like everyone here has already fallen into groups. I don't care, not really. Still, it would be nice to have at least one person here.

"Chloe!"

I barely manage to repress a groan. I've been here all of five hours, yet that voice is already way too familiar.

"Hi, Mara," I say. I do some quick thinking. I look down at my stick. All the marshmallows have roasted perfectly. "I promised my friend I'd bring her a marshmallow, but I'll talk to you later, okay?"

"Can't wait!" she says.

Ugh. She thinks we're, like, actual friends. I'll have to figure out how to deal with that later. In the meantime, I guess I should actually act like I have a friend who wants a marshmallow. My eyes land on Maddie. She's sitting on a stone bench about ten feet away. No one is sitting next to her.

This is probably a bad idea, but I don't have a choice. Besides . . . maybe a marshmallow could work as a peace offering. I might as well give it a try.

I walk up to her, extending the marshmallows.

"You don't have one," I say.

In the dim light, I can't quite make out Maddie's face. But I know her. I'm pretty sure that she's scowling.

"No, thanks," she says.

Yeah, okay. This was so not a good idea. But I'm committed to the part now.

"Are you sure, Mads? I roasted it just the way you like it."

That part is true. Maddie and I both like our marshmallows the same way: golden brown, no hints of black. So, while I may not have intended to give Maddie one of my marshmallows, exactly, it works out.

I think she's going to refuse me again, but she doesn't. Maddie takes the stick and starts in on one of the marshmallows.

"How do you know I like my marshmallows like this?" she asks when she's done chewing.

Not a question I expected. I shrug. "Remember the fourth-grade camping trip? Before the pandemic and everything?"

"Right." Maddie looks down. "I guess I didn't expect you to remember something like that."

I want to ask why not. I do remember things about my best friend! Well, former best friend.

Maddie leans in toward the marshmallow stick. Before she can take another bite, she drops it. The entire thing slides straight into the mud.

"Ack, sorry!" I say. "Do you want me to get another one for you?"

She stands up from the bench with pursed lips and narrowed eyes.

"Don't bother," she says.

And then she sprints away from me.

Again.

Maddie

I should have known this was a terrible idea. I should have known that twelve is too old for birthday parties.

Unluckily, Chloe convinced me otherwise. "It'll be sooo fun," she said. I could have a real, grown-up birthday party, not one of those silly kids' parties with clowns and pin the tail on the donkey. If anyone knows how to be cool, it's Chloe. So I decided to follow her suggestion. (Why do I always follow her suggestions?)

She approved the entire plan. Mom and Sandra reserved the back room at Johnny's, my very favorite pizza shop. We would not play games or do any of that kid stiff. Chloe said we could just "mingle." Even though mingling isn't really my favorite thing, I knew it would be okay. Because Chloe would be there to help everything along, to cover up for my being quiet and awkward and, well, *me*.

After all, Chloe has never not been to my birthday, ever since I turned eight and she was the only one who showed up.

She sends her text an hour before the party is supposed to begin.

Maddie, I'm sooooo sorry.

When I see the message, my heart leaps into my throat and dances around my trachea for good measure. Even though Chloe's message is vague, I know what's happening, and I don't like it.

I text her back.

What's going on?

A minute later, she replies.

I can't come to your party. ☹ Have to go redo stuff for the commercial.

Soooo sorry.

Tugging at my hair, I let out a breath through my teeth. The period medicine commercial? Chloe didn't even want to do that in the first place! I saw her face when her mother delivered the news. She hasn't really talked about it since, but I know how much she hates the whole situation. And now she's missing my birthday party—the party she told me to have!—so she can pretend to be sick on camera.

All of it is enough to make *me* sick, truly. Sick with nerves and panic and . . . and something else, too. Something that feels an awful lot like rage.

Why didn't Chloe just tell her mother no, that they should reschedule for another day? a voice whispers in my ear. Maybe the voice rises into more than a whisper. I shouldn't have these thoughts, but I do.

After all, for 364 days a year Chloe can do her commercials and auditions and be the perfect child actor her mother wants. But I only have one birthday: today.

Right now.

I want to send her a text full of swear words and angry faces, but I don't. That's not something that nice, supportive Maddie would do. It most definitely is not what Chloe wants from her best friend. I know that, of course. So I hold back my emotions when I respond, just like I always do.

I get it. Break a leg!

After I hit send, I grind my teeth so hard I ache. Now I somehow need to scrounge up enough energy to survive my own birthday party. A party I never even wanted in the first place.

I do not speak to my moms on the drive to Johnny's. The nerves overwhelm me, blocking out any desire to form actual words.

Even though I don't want the car ride to end, it does. We arrive at Johnny's, and a nice waiter ushers us into the special room. A huge silver banner hangs on the wall: HAPPY BIRTHDAY MADDIE.

I try to keep my face blank and free of grimaces, but I fail.

One by one, the guests enter. Most of them are girls from school who I barely know. I invited them because I needed to invite someone. And because Chloe suggested it.

"Hi," I say to each of them in turn. "Thank you for coming to my party."

After I do that, I cannot manage to say much of anything. The girls do what people usually do at parties, I guess, and talk with one another. I might as well not exist. I try to pretend it doesn't matter, but it does. Of course it does.

When the waiter finally brings out the pizza, relief washes over me. At least no one will expect me to talk while I'm eating. Except . . . except everyone else keeps talking even though the pizza is right here. My own slice—sausage and spinach, my favorite—is soggy cardboard in my mouth.

After two flavorless pieces, I absolutely cannot stand it

41

any longer. I rush to the bathroom. True, I don't really need to go, but I would take any excuse to get out of that room. Away from all the people who are not and never will be my friends.

The bathroom is just a bathroom, and not even a particularly nice one. But right now, it's a refuge. I glance at my watch and debate how long I can possibly stay in here without raising suspicions. Ten minutes would be pushing it, but probably okay.

But ten minutes comes and goes, and sometime around minute twelve, I hear the voices. I can't put a name to them, but I know with absolute certainty that they're my guests. The girls Chloe likes. (Does she like them more than she likes me?)

"Gah," one of them says. "What a sucky party."

"I know, right? Why did we even come?"

My face burns. I am very, very grateful for the thin door of the bathroom stall separating me from them.

"You know why we came," the first girl says. "To hang out with Chloe Winters."

A loud sigh scratches against my ears before the other girl responds. "Yeah, I know. Bad idea. Chloe isn't even here!"

"Probably couldn't stand to be around her boring, fat friend anymore."

And with that they both break into giggles. Because, I guess, that is funny.

Stupid, obnoxious tears well up behind my eyes. I try and try to stop them, but I can't. Their words keep looping around and around in my head.

Fat. Boring. Friend.

Of course, I know that I have a body most people would describe as "fat"—maybe "plump" or "round" if they're trying to be nice. I've heard it all. Mostly I try not to let being fat bother me, and mostly I succeed. Not always, but usually. What bothers me more is other people's reactions to me. As though I am less than because I am fat.

I can handle someone else calling me fat, but being called *boring* somehow cuts deeper. Does Chloe think I'm boring? She doesn't. She couldn't. I'm almost sure of it. But before today, I was sure that she would never, ever, not in a million years miss my birthday party.

As I wipe tears away from my traitorous eyes, I check my phone for new messages. Chloe's name pops up, and I tap to read her text.

Hope the party is super fun!!! Just remember to smile and talk to people and don't get too caught up in your head, okay? Love you!

I scowl at my phone.

"Thanks for the advice, Chloe," I mutter to no one.

Chloe

"So, what do you think?" I ask.

Maddie blinks at me.

"What do I think about what?"

Since Maddie is my best friend, I don't roll my eyes at her. Well, okay, maybe I do. But only a little! In response to the question, I show her two tops I like: one turquoise and sparkly, the other purple satin.

"Which one should I get?"

"That one," Maddie says, pointing to the purple one.

I'm pretty sure she just picked at random. Which doesn't help my dilemma at all.

Still, I think about it. The purple is pretty, but it doesn't match my hair. Cordelia always says that we redheads have to be very careful about our colors. I add the turquoise blouse to my pile.

Since it's the weekend after Thanksgiving, the store is packed. We need to pay and get out of here before the next bajillion years pass. With my pile of clothes teetering in my arms, I march to the checkout line. That's when I notice that Maddie isn't carrying anything.

"You didn't like anything here? Seriously?" I ask.

"Nope."

"Why not? I saw some really cute skirts and I think they'd look gre—"

"Chloe," Maddie interrupts me. I stare at her. Maddie never interrupts me. Well, almost never. "I can't shop at this store."

"What? Why?"

I'm honestly confused here. This isn't an expensive store, and anyway, Maddie's family has more money than mine does. Cordelia doesn't make a ton of money in her job as a receptionist, and she makes me save the money I earn acting. So I just don't get what the problem is here.

Maddie stares at me. "You really don't know?"

"Uh, yeah, that's what I said."

She crosses her arms over her chest. "I just don't like anything."

I shrug. The whole situation is kind of weird, but if that's what Maddie wants to do, fine. It's not my problem. Like, I don't have psychic powers. How am I supposed to know what she thinks if she won't tell me?

Half an hour later, we finally make it through the check-out line. I glance at my watch. There's still more than an hour before Maddie's mom is coming to pick us up. We could do another store. Too bad Maddie isn't in a shopping kind of mood.

I figure that Maddie should pick the next thing we do. But we've walked halfway down a fake street of the outdoor mall before I realize that Maddie is just following my lead.

So I look around for something to do. Anything, really. Most of the options are not great. A fancy sunglasses shop. An electronics store. A smoothie place with a line winding out the door. No, thanks.

Then I see it. A bright yellow sign: HAIRCUTS 50% OFF.

The salon is full of cheap plastic chairs and checkerboard floor tiles. Yeah, that's the kind of place Cordelia would never, ever visit. Also, it's completely empty.

I grab Maddie's arm and point.

"You want to get a haircut?" she asks, eyebrow raised. "Now?"

I pause. This is a big decision, for sure. But . . .

"Yeah," I say. "I do."

I tug at my hair. It's almost waist length. I've wanted a haircut since forever, but Cordelia wants to wait until my usual stylist gets back from having a baby. Because I guess going to another hairdresser will result in a hair-tastrophe.

Cordelia would be so mad if she knew I was even considering this. I kind of love that.

As I turn back to Maddie, I can see the thoughts spinning through her head. She knows just as well as I do that Cordelia would be super not happy about my plan.

But Cordelia isn't here.

Maddie gives me a small smile. "Sure. Let's do it."

I feel very grown up as I walk to the desk in front of the salon.

"Hello," I say. "We'll take two haircuts, please."

The guy at the desk squints, like he's trying to place me. Side effect of being sort-of famous. But if he recognizes me, he doesn't say so.

"Right this way, ladies," he tells us.

My heartbeat picks up a bit as we follow him to the spinny chairs.

Maddie squeezes my hand. "If I end up bald, it's all your fault," she says.

I relax my shoulders a bit. "You'd look great bald, Mads," I tell her.

Maddie opens her mouth to reply, but we don't have time to talk. The guy points us toward two chairs, each with a smiling stylist. We are getting haircuts.

I face myself in the mirror as I put on one of those ugly black robes. The stylist—a cool-looking woman with turquoise-streaked hair—spins my chair around. "What do you want today, doll?"

Part of me wants to ask for a colored streak like hers. Purple, maybe. Then I remember that purple is Not My Color. Besides, I'm feeling brave, but not *that* brave.

"I'd like you to cut my hair, please," I say. My voice shakes. "Ear length."

Next to me, Maddie makes a surprised noise. I try to ignore it.

"You sure about that, deary?" the stylist asks me.

No, Cordelia's voice says in my head. *Absolutely not, Chloe Winters. Your hair is your signature.*

I smile brightly. "I'm sure."

As the stylist snip-snips away at my hair, I try to stay calm. I try not to think too hard about the red locks piling up on the floor behind me. I know, I just know, that if I allow myself to dwell on it, I might panic.

Too late to go back now, anyway.

"Take a look," the stylist finally announces.

I stare at my reflection. I'm still there—my narrow chin, my green eyes, my sharp cheekbones. But it also isn't me. The short hair makes me look older. Cooler. More grown up.

And the best part? I don't look like the girl who starred in *Super Hero Kids* for three seasons.

"I love it," I tell the stylist. "Thank you so much."

Her shoulders relax and she beams at me.

Oh, Cordelia is going to hate this. Like, really, really hate this.

"You look great," Maddie says when she sees me. "You're all sophisticated."

I grin. "You look fabulous, too."

She smiles back and pats her curly brown hair, now several inches shorter. "Thanks."

Then I offer her my arm. We leave the salon with our elbows interlocked, and I feel so fancy. In that moment, with Maddie by my side, I can almost forget about my mother.

I more or less float through the rest of our time at the mall, stuck in a new-haircut haze. Maybe I'm vain, but I don't care. I try to catch a glimpse of myself in every store window we pass. Just to check that yeah, I still have short hair. I feel like a whole new Chloe.

When Maddie's mom picks us up, I can tell that our spur-of-the-moment haircuts surprise her. She compliments both of us, though. Gah. Maddie is so lucky.

On the way back, we run into the predictably bad Los Angeles traffic. Sitting in the back of the car gives me way too much time to think about things I'd rather not. Long as

this ride home is, part of me hopes that it never ends. Cordelia just might snap when she sees me.

"Chlo," Maddie says to me when her mom drops me off. "Just . . . good luck, okay? And I'm here if you want to talk."

I nod. I can't think of another response to Maddie's niceness. Not when a fight with Cordelia is looming.

I trudge up the pathway to our apartment building. Just a few minutes ago, Cordelia's opinion on my hair didn't matter at all. Now, it's all I can think about.

Ugh. Just get it over with, Chloe.

I walk into our apartment to find Cordelia lounging on the couch. She scrolls through her phone.

"Hi, hon."

Cordelia doesn't look up. So I clear my throat. Finally, my mom looks at me. And she lets out an actual gasp.

"Chloe! What happened?"

She asks the question as if I returned bruised and bloody.

I shrug. *Keep it casual, self.* If I act like it's no big deal, maybe it won't be a big deal. Knowing Cordelia, it won't be a small deal. It can't. But maybe I can hope for a medium-sized deal.

Ha.

"I thought it was time for a change," I say.

Cordelia lets out a choking sound. "Okay, so you're doing the preteen rebellion thing. I get it. I've read the books. But, Chloe, did it have to be *this*? Can't you just start wearing black?"

My heart thumps painfully in my chest.

"It's just a temporary thing. Hair grows back," I say finally. I rehearsed so many arguments in my head, but this is all I can think to say.

49

"You have two auditions next month."

Her voice is getting sharper. I try not to cringe.

I know she wants me to beg for her forgiveness, but I don't. And the madder she gets, the more certain I feel. It was *my* hair. I had every right to make my decision.

"How is my acting going to be hurt by the length of my hair?" I ask.

Cordelia closes her eyes and lets out a loud breath. "Chloe, we've talked about this before. It's not your hair, it's your im—"

"My image! I know. But . . . but I like it. Why can't my image be a girl with short hair?"

Another Cordelia-sized sigh. "Hollywood isn't forgiving. You know this. People might think you're . . . you know."

She trails off, and I frown. "What will they think?"

"That you're . . . you know. A lesbian. Or something. Not that there's anything wrong with that. But it's not the image we want to project, right?"

I just nod. If I try to speak, I'm sure that only gibberish will come out.

Once she dismisses me, I race to my room. I put my headphones in and start playing *Guys and Dolls* at top volume. Slowly—very, very slowly—the music works its magic. Cordelia's words stop repeating themselves in my head.

Well, mostly.

My phone pings with a text message. Maddie.

How are you?

I don't text her back.

50

CHAPTER FIVE

Maddie

NOW: JULY

I stare at the printout of my schedule that appeared on my bed after breakfast this morning. For something like the tenth time, I read it. I can't help but hope that the words have magically changed since read number nine. They have not.

I close my eyes and take several slow, deliberate breaths. That's what Sandra tells me to do when I get anxious. It sort of works. My heartbeat slows down ever so slightly. But I still have a ginormous problem, and I know I won't be okay until everything is fixed.

Chewing on the inside of my lip, I search for Audrey. She's at the other end of the cabin, talking with a brown-haired girl whose name I don't remember. Audrey gives the girl a wide smile. Clearly, she doesn't know she just ruined my summer and quite possibly my entire life.

My hands jitter in my pockets as I approach her. She's still talking to the other girl.

If I were in a movie, Audrey would just know that I have something terribly important to tell her. She would shoo Other Girl away—nicely, of course—and ask me what I need. But in real life, Other Girl talks for forever.

"Hey, Maddie," Audrey says once Other Girl has finally skipped off. "What's going on?"

"There's been a mistake." I wave my schedule in the air.

"Right!" Audrey smacks herself in the forehead, reminding me of a hammy actor in a bad sitcom. "I wanted to talk with you about this last night. I tried to find you at the campfire, but I couldn't, and by the time I got back to the cabin you were asleep."

The truth is, I had not been sleeping. After my encounter with Chloe, I curled myself in my sleeping bag so I could avoid talking to anyone else. But better for Audrey to think I'm an early sleeper than just plain pathetic.

After taking in a large gulp of air, I try to straighten out my panicky thoughts. "There's only one screenwriting class on my schedule," I say in a wavering voice. "That . . . that's just a mistake. You printed out the wrong schedule or something. Right?"

Audrey flashes a smile tinged with pity. No, no, and no.

I want to run out of this scene.

"I'm really sorry to be the bearer of bad news, Maddie. But our screenwriting instructor had to cancel at the last minute. She got called to fill in as a writer on a new TV show. It's about flight attendants who are actually superspies. Or something. I'm a little vague on the details. Anyway, a new streaming service wants it, so she had to go."

I could not possibly be less interested in superspy flight attendants. I guess Audrey realizes this, because she quickly moves on. "Hannah really tried. She did her best to find another screenwriting instructor, but no one was available on such short notice."

I can almost feel my heart spiraling through my rib cage.

My throat feels very dry when I finally speak. "There . . . there isn't anyone else? Anyone at all?"

Audrey sighs. "I'm afraid not. But the good news is that we're doing a screenwriting elective. You're signed up for that! Hannah will be leading it herself, and let me tell you—she's an awesome teacher. Plus, you'll get to try acting!"

"But . . . but . . ." I try to come up with something clever to say and fail completely. I guess there isn't really anything I can say. It isn't as if Audrey or Hannah or anyone else can go back in time and convince the TV people that a show about superspy flight attendants is a terrible idea. Even though it really, really is.

"I know it sucks," Audrey says. Her face twists into a sympathetic expression. "But I really do think this could be a supercool opportunity, you know? So many great screenwriters and directors started out as actors."

She starts to go on about Greta Gerwig's career. I don't bother telling Audrey that I most definitely will not be a Gerwig. After the school musical disaster . . . well, it's just obvious, isn't it?

Maybe you could still be an actor, a tiny voice nags at me from some rarely used corner of my mind. Maybe, just maybe, this can be my second chance. My chance to be a star, just like Chloe.

Oh, shut up, voice. I try to clear my head of such nonsense and focus on the conversation at hand.

"I don't want to write musicals or plays," I say. "I want to write movies and TV."

Audrey nods. "I get it. But you can learn a lot from working on a musical. It's a chance to expand your horizons!"

Of course she would say something like that.

"If I have to act, do I have to be in the musical like my schedule says?" I manage to get out. My voice croaks far more than I'd like. "Can't I . . . can't I do the play instead?"

Audrey nods. "If you want, sure. They're doing Shakespeare—*Taming of the Shrew*. You know that one?"

I frown as I try to process all of this. I think back to the *Shakespeare for Kids* book Sandra gave me for my tenth birthday. When I start to remember the plot, I make a face. "Isn't that one really sexist?"

"No arguments from me on that one," Audrey says. "It totally is. But hey, if that's what you want, I'm sure we could make it happen."

Chewing on my lip, I shift my weight from one foot to another. I could either be in a boring, sexist Shakespeare play . . . or . . . or I could do the musical.

I should go for the Shakespeare, I know. And yet something stops me from saying it.

Audrey must sense my uncertainty, because she gives me a sympathetic smile. "I know musicals are scary, but I promise you that it will be super fun. I'm in charge this year. I care about finding every actor a role that allows them to thrive."

Of course, I understand what Audrey means. She thinks I can't handle having a big part in the musical. The worst part is, she's right. I proved that back in May. If I am going to do this musical, I need a small part. A safe part. Maybe a tree? Every musical needs trees.

A horrible thought creeps up on me.

"Will I have to dance?" I ask.

Audrey's smile tightens. "Well, every role is different. But yeah. Usually most people dance in the musical."

The news is so horrifying that I cannot even summon a response.

My moms would tell me that I should let Audrey know about my dyspraxia and what it means. Maybe even tell her what happened at school, if she doesn't know. But she already thinks I'm pathetic, probably, and I would prefer not to keep revealing the depths of my pathetic-ness. Besides, a lot of people don't even believe me when I talk about my disability. It can kind of feel like there isn't much point to saying anything. So I don't bother with it.

I could be in the stupid Shakespeare play. Or maybe ask if I can go home, even. The program I signed up for isn't happening. Why should I have to stay here and suffer?

I should do one of those things. I should. Yet I just can't help but feel it would be, I don't know, cowardly.

"Okay," I say in a very small voice. "I guess . . . I guess I'll do the musical."

CHAPTER SIX

Chloe

The thing about auditions is that there are a bunch of unwritten rules. The biggest one: Don't look at the competition. But I don't bother with the unwritten rules. I always look.

Auditions are in the same barn we used for last night's talent show, so the stage is familiar. Usually I don't get that kind of advantage.

I start evaluating the competition the moment I find a front-row seat. Obviously it's not like I can judge people's talent just by looking at them. Still, I'm not impressed. A bunch of kids are throwing a Frisbee around at the back of the barn. Hello, people! We're not auditioning for the sports-no-one-cares-about club. This is serious.

Closing my eyes, I begin the set of breathing exercises my old vocal coach taught me, before Cordelia decided to stop the lessons. Next, I move into my voice warm-ups. When I open my eyes, a whole crowd of kids are staring at me. Okay. Fine. Let them look.

One of them is the pretty girl from the cabin. The one who danced like no one was watching. Then, another familiar face. Maddie. My palms sweat. I definitely didn't expect *her* to be here.

She's standing about ten feet away, but I don't even think about it. My feet automatically carry me toward her.

"What are you doing here?" I ask.

Her face twists into a scowl, and in my mind I wince. Lately I always seem to say the wrong thing when it comes to Maddie.

"I'm going to be in the musical," Maddie says. Most people wouldn't notice, but her voice shakes a bit. "Why else would I be here?"

She puts her hands in her pockets and fiddles with them.

Okay. She's not happy about this development. That makes two of us. I don't need a distraction. Not today, with everything on the line.

I try to find something to say that doesn't sound mean. "I thought you were doing the screenwriting program."

"I thought so, too." She crosses her arms over her chest. "It's canceled. So here I am."

As I process this information, I try not to frown. Maddie being in the musical was definitely not part of my plan. But whatever. It shouldn't matter. It doesn't matter.

"That's, uh, too bad. But it's good to have you here, and I'm sure you'll do fine," I tell her.

Two lies in as many sentences. Bad, I know. But I don't know what else to say, and I should try to be nice, maybe.

Another scowl from Maddie. "I hope you can act better than that for your audition."

"I wasn't acting!" I say.

But I am, sort of. Before, when everything was good between us, I never had to act around Maddie. Now? Different story.

57

Just as Maddie opens her mouth to respond, Audrey's voice blares through the room.

"Welcome, cast!" she says.

And just like that, I'm saved. I turn my attention toward the stage, where it belongs. I try to forget all about Maddie.

"I'm sure you've all been wondering what musical we are going to be performing this summer," Audrey says. "You don't need to wonder anymore. I am thrilled to announce that we will be performing . . . wait, excuse me. I need a prop."

Out of nowhere, Audrey pulls out a hat. A black, pointy hat. I can't help but let out a very uncool squeal. Does this mean what I think it does?

"Yes, that's right, people! We will be performing the modern classic you all know and love, a tale of a friendship and betrayal and heartbreak. Get ready to begin the Camp Rosewood production of . . . *Wicked*!"

With another flourish of her hands, Audrey breaks into song: "No One Mourns The Wicked." I clap my hands together. For once, I don't care if I look a little silly. This is it! My big chance.

I am going to be Elphaba. I just have to.

Just as I start to think about my audition strategy, I remember my ex–best friend sitting next to me. Maddie is practically turning green herself. She makes a pained noise. I consider trying to comfort her, I really do . . . but I don't move. Maddie could not possibly make it any more clear that she doesn't want my help.

I retreat into a corner to continue my voice warm-ups. I try to focus all of my energy on Elphaba. But even as I review the songs in my head, Maddie's face never really leaves me.

Once auditions start for real, I've just about managed to tune out all the extra stuff floating around in my head. The annoying stuff. I focus on my real goal: Elphaba.

Most of the other kids are not great. They're better than the kids back home, but not by much.

Then, *the* girl walks onto the stage. The girl from my cabin who . . . caught my attention with her dancing yesterday. But, okay, whatever. That doesn't mean she can sing.

She . . . whoever she is . . . opens her mouth. And belts out a more-than-good rendition of "The Wizard And I." I straighten myself in my chair. Okay, so there are talented people here after all. That's good. But no way is this girl an actual threat to me. She just isn't.

Toward the end of the final chorus, the girl wobbles just a little bit off pitch. Flat, which means the note wasn't as high as it should have been. Most people probably wouldn't even notice, but I do.

Even though the bad note grates against my ears, I smile. Too bad for her.

Still. She recovers from the mistake and finishes off by holding a superlong note. Thanks to the room's acoustics, the note rings through the air for moments after she closes her mouth.

Hmmph. So. This girl is talented in addition to being

pretty. I can only hope she's a terrible actor. But, for some reason, I don't think she is.

"Thank you, Sasha," Audrey says, looking up from her clipboard.

So that's the girl's name—Sasha. She does look like a Sasha. Which is a ridiculous thought, because how do you look like a name? I don't think I look much like a Chloe.

Sasha sways her hips as she walks off the stage. She's a little on the curvy side. Cordelia would say she needs to lose fifteen pounds to have a chance at a lead role. I don't think that at all. My eyes follow her all the way as she glides back to her chair, like there's a spotlight following her around.

I snap myself out of whatever weirdness came over me. I have to think about my own audition. There are still four singers to go before I take my turn. Back at the beginning of the day, when Audrey sent the sign-up sheet around, picking the final audition slot seemed smart. Leave the best for last, right? Now I seriously regret my decision. I just want the whole thing over with.

I don't even want to think about what Cordelia might say if I don't get Elphaba. If I fail.

Not going to happen. Even if Sasha is talented and pretty and . . . Why am I thinking so much about Sasha again? I need to think about me. Maybe this is just a camp musical, but it's still a big opportunity. My chance to show Cordelia that I can choose my own roles, thank you very much.

A few more kids do their auditions. Most sing off-key.

Ugh. Why do people who can't sing try to sing? Don't they know how painful it is for the rest of us?

Right before it's my turn, Maddie sings. Her voice is quiet but steady. She really is a better singer than she knows.

"Good job," I tell her while she shuffles off the stage.

She doesn't even bother responding to me. Rude.

But I can't think about Maddie. It's my turn.

I march up to the microphone and announce my full name, just like I do at real auditions. And I sing.

I decide not to sing "Defying Gravity" again. Cordelia always says it's important to show range. On this, I agree with her. So I sing "Goodnight, My Someone" from *The Music Man*. I could pretty much perform it in my sleep at this point, after I played Marian in our school's musical this spring. The song fits my voice perfectly, and has room for me to show off in just the right ways.

My voice shakes a little at the beginning, but I push past it. I always do.

As I sing, I try to forget about being Chloe. I want to be Marian, the lonely librarian in Iowa. But even as my voice soars, I can't forget about Chloe problems. Not 100 percent. I'm still wondering if Maddie will ever be not mad at me and why I can't stop thinking about Sasha and also what will Cordelia say if I fail and . . .

I finish the song. Hopefully I didn't show any of my thoughts. Audrey gives me a nod, and I try not to frown. What does that even mean? I try not to dwell on it as I return to my seat.

"Good audition."

I spin around in search of the new voice. It's Sasha, looking right at me with a shy smile.

Why is she here? If this is some kind of attempt to intimidate me, it's not going to work. I smile back at her, wide enough to show my teeth.

"Thank you," I say in my most gracious voice. "You were great, too."

Sasha only shrugs. For the longest time, she doesn't say anything else. Annoying! I don't actually want to talk with her, obviously. Still. If she's just going to stand here, I might as well try to get some useful information out of her.

I try not to think about how pretty her brown eyes are.

"So. What part do you want?" I ask.

Yeah, not very subtle. But I have to find out, and I don't have the patience for subtle.

Sasha smiles, again.

"Why do you ask?" she says, as if she doesn't know perfectly well what I'm doing.

"I was just thinking you'd be a great Galinda," I tell her. It's sort of true.

"And what if I want to be Elphaba?" she says, eyebrows arched in a clear challenge.

"Then I'd say good luck beating me to it."

At that, Sasha laughs. My cheeks heat up. People never laugh at me. Except, apparently, her.

"Well, Chloe Winters, *I'd* say you're in for a little competition."

Then she turns away, leaving me more confused than ever.

I can feel my cheeks heating up and it's so uncomfortable and then I look around to make sure no one noticed. Maddie is still staring at me, but she won't meet my gaze. No one else is paying any attention. I allow myself a relieved sigh.

What is *happening* to me?

Maddie

Chloe pounces on me the moment I enter the cafeteria.

"Mads! Best news ever. They're doing *The Music Man*!"

I frown. For a moment, I can't quite figure out what she means. Then I get it: the school musical. Our school must be doing *The Music Man* this year. Chloe has made sure I know all the musical theater classics from our movie nights, so I must have seen it before.

When I remember the story, I make a face. "That one?" I ask. "The supposedly heartwarming story of how a con artist tricked an entire town into giving him money? And then, for some reason, they end up thanking him for it? While the smart girl gives up her independence so she can marry him?"

Chloe waves her hand to the side, as though what I said could not possibly be less relevant. I guess it couldn't be, to her.

"Yeah, yeah, I know. But seriously, Mads, when are you going to learn that plot is the least important part of a musical?"

I shake my head. Chloe and I have had this argument about four zillion times. I always say that plot is the most important part of any story—and one hundred years of screenwriting wisdom back me up on this point. That is just a fact. But Chloe, for some reason, thinks otherwise. She says that musicals are different. According to her, they're all about "the spectacle"—the music, the dancing, the costumes. My counterargument is that musicals should have a plot, at least a little, because otherwise we end up with *Cats*. At which point Chloe shakes her head and we agree to disagree.

Today I decide to skip the whole debate. We slide into our usual lunch table and open our lunch bags. As I bite into my roast beef sandwich, I notice that five girls have gathered at the end of our table—not close to us, exactly, but close enough. I'd bet anything they're here so they can gawk at Chloe.

I call these people groupies, but whenever I mention it to Chloe she gets annoyed. She sees them, though. I can tell by the way her shoulders tense up, the way she chews more vigorously on her apple slices. But she doesn't say anything about the groupies' unwanted presence, so neither do I. Instead, I return to the troublesome subject of *The Music Man*.

"You want the librarian part, I guess?" I ask. That is the most important role for a girl, and I wouldn't expect Chloe to want anything else.

"Well, obviously! I've definitely got the range." Chloe pauses. "How about you?"

I nearly choke on my sandwich. For a rather long moment, I wait for it to finish going down my throat the right way. Finally, once I feel certain I am safe from death by lettuce, I speak again.

"I will be watching you from the audience. I'll give you a standing ovation. I promise."

Yet even as I say it, I feel my stomach twist. The very idea of me performing in the school musical is ridiculous. Laughable, in truth. And yet . . . and yet part of me wonders. Could I do it? Could I even be good at it?

I know the answers to these questions. I should not even be considering this. The school musical is for girls like Chloe, not girls like me. I probably couldn't even do all the complicated dance moves, with my dyspraxia and everything that comes with it. Sometimes I struggle even to tell the difference between left and right. Still, a voice whispers to me. *Maybe.*

Shaking myself, I turn my attention back to Chloe. For some reason she droops with disappointment, almost as if she actually cares about me being in the musical.

"And that's it? You'll just watch from the audience?" she asks.

I shrug. "What else would I do?"

She's not actually suggesting that I join the musical myself, is she? Because that would be ridiculous.

"You could be onstage with me," Chloe says, in her most earnest voice.

My hands grip the edge of the cafeteria table so hard that it digs into my skin. I cannot believe that Chloe just said that, of all things. How does she even know about my wish? My silly and impossible wish, which maybe is not so impossible after all.

I should not even be considering this, and yet I am. That's the thing about Chloe. Somehow, by the sheer force of her Chloe-ness, she gets me to consider things I'd never

even think about if not for her putting the idea in my head. Chloe's ideas are usually an itch I can't quite scratch away. Sometimes this is the best thing about being friends with her, and sometimes it's the absolute worst.

"No," I say. "Absolutely not. And also . . . no."

Chloe clucks her tongue. "Mads! You can do it. You can sing!"

From her, that is quite the compliment. And I want to believe her, I do, but I just can't.

"Sure. I can sing in the car when a good song comes on. I can sing in the shower. But I can't—I repeat, *can't*—do it onstage in front of the entire school."

That is just a fact, no different from saying that the sky is blue or that Hawkeye is the worst Avenger. Some things are just that obvious. I really do not know where Chloe got this weird idea about me being in the musical, but sooner or later she will realize how very ridiculous it is.

Unfortunately, that moment is not now.

"Please?" she whines. "Pretty pretty please?"

I frown. I don't want to be suspicious of her, but usually when Chloe wants me to do something this much, there is something in it for her.

"Why do you want me to humiliate myself so badly?" I ask, crossing my arms.

"You are not going to humiliate yourself!"

I stare down at the linoleum table. "I'm not good with . . . you know, dancing things."

Chloe knows about my dyspraxia. I didn't exactly want to tell her, but when I somehow managed to sprain my ankle

while crossing the street, I decided that some explanation was necessary.

Still, there's a difference between knowing and actually believing me. Sometimes it feels like she thinks I'm just making it up or something. As though I can somehow not have dyspraxia if I really, really work at it.

She doesn't understand. How could she?

Chloe's face twitches, but she just waves a hand again. "You worry too much, Mads. You'll be fine."

I grind my teeth. Now more than ever, I am absolutely convinced there's something she has failed to mention.

"Just tell me what you want," I say. I am very proud of myself for managing to be all forceful and everything.

"Okay, okay . . . so, I kind of need you to do this. For me."

The very idea that Chloe needs me—really and truly *needs* me—fills me with a warm glow, at first. Then the more sensible part of my brain assumes control, and I clench my fists. Typical Chloe. When she feels like it, she misses my birthday party and gives me useless advice and doesn't bother texting me back. But now, when she actually needs something from me, here she is being nice.

"Why do you need me?" I ask. Because I deserve to know that much, at least.

And then you'll do what she wants, won't you, because that's what you always do, a voice whispers. I ignore it. Mostly.

Chloe stares at her sandwich. "My mom doesn't want me taking the bus too late. And, you know, her work schedule means she can't pick me up from rehearsal every day. But if you did the musical, your moms could drive me home."

Ah. So that explains it. Chloe wants me to suffer in exchange for rides. She plans to use me, again. Well, what if I say no?

But then I turn to her and she looks at me with wide, pleading eyes. Any angry words I might have summoned dissolve in my throat.

"Please, Maddie?" she says. "I really, really want this. It will be fun, I swear. I wouldn't ask you to do this if it weren't going to be fun for you, too."

Chewing on the inside of my mouth, I try to search for a solution to the situation. Something that will make Chloe happy without me risking total humiliation. There has got to be some kind of answer to this, something that does not involve me getting onstage.

"The crew!" I say. "Maybe I can be in the crew? Like painting sets and all of that."

In all honesty, the idea of spending hours after school painting trees really doesn't fill me with joy, and I certainly don't have any talent for it. But at least being on the crew doesn't involve *dancing*.

Chloe wrinkles her nose, as if I just suggested my desire to wade through a bug-infested pond. "Really, Mads? The crew?"

"Why not?"

She leans forward. Her face is still positioned in a perfect pout. "Come on! That's so boring. Don't you want to do something that's actually important? We could be onstage together!"

I close my eyes and let out a long breath. So many scenes

play out in my mind—me, tripping onstage. Freezing up when it's time to deliver a line. Yet those aren't the only images I see. There's also a roaring crowd, standing to give me an ovation. Not Chloe, but me. Maddie Simmons.

I should not even be considering this. But in the end, I can only give Chloe one response.

"Fine. I'll do it."

"Really?" Chloe positively squeals. "Oh my gosh, thank you, thank you, thank you! Mads, you're the best friend ever."

I smile at the rush of compliments. But even now, I can feel my sandwich churning around in my poor stomach. I just agreed to be in the school musical.

Because you can never just say no to her, a voice whispers. *You're pathetic.*

I try my very best to ignore it.

Chloe

Today is *it*. Cast announcement day.

I try not to skip as I make my way over to the music room, where Ms. Wilkinson will post the cast list. Chloe Winters does not skip. But if I maybe walk a little faster than usual . . . well, I hope I don't look too uncool.

Nobody else is there when I reach the door. Weird. Really, doesn't everyone else know that today is the big day?

For a moment, I worry that maybe Ms. W forgot to put up the list. But nope, it's right there. I dance on my toes as I search for my name. I find it soon enough. CHLOE WINTERS AS MARIAN PAROO.

I squeal.

Honestly, I don't know what I would have done if I hadn't been cast as Marian. Given that the level of musical talent at Pasadena Middle School is not, shall we say, very high, missing out on the lead part would have been the most embarrassing thing ever.

Now I don't have to worry about that. I did it. I am going to be Marian. I almost start belting out "Seventy-Six Trombones" in celebration.

I have a part. An important part, one that has nothing to do with cramps.

Just as I start walking away from the music room and the

ever-important cast list, I realize I should check the rest of the list. I want to know about Maddie. And maybe everyone else in the cast, too.

The role of Harold Hill is going to Carlos Luna, a boy I know a little from my classes. That makes sense. Only a handful of boys even auditioned for the musical, and Carlos was the only one who could hold a tune. He wasn't as good as, well, me. Still. I can share a stage with him.

All of a sudden, it occurs to me that I won't just be onstage with Carlos. I'll have to act as though I am falling in love with him. Harold and Marian even share a kiss. I make a face at the thought. Nothing against Carlos, but I've never kissed a boy. Now I'll have to do it in front of *everyone*.

Frowning, I think about who I might like to kiss onstage. Not Carlos. Not any of the other boys in my grade, for sure. But if not them, then who?

Ugh, I don't want to think about that. I search for Maddie's name on the list. There it is—MADDIE SIMMONS AS MRS. PAROO. Maddie will be playing my mother.

Huh. Mrs. Paroo is a good part, actually. That makes sense. Maddie can sing, no matter how much she protests otherwise. And I know she can memorize lines, because she knows at least half a dozen superhero movies by heart.

Great. Everything is working out just as I planned. I'm going to be the star. Maddie will be, if not a star exactly, then at least a supporting player. Okay, so maybe she wasn't exactly thrilled about being in the musical, but once we

actually start rehearsals she'll change her mind. It'll be fun for her. I know it.

I almost dance to my first-period social studies class, my happiness outweighing the need to look cool. Since there are still ten minutes until class starts, most people are just hanging out in the hallways. They don't realize that I just got the biggest news of my life. Or at least the last two months. Doesn't matter. I don't feel like talking to them. Then I see Maddie and wave.

"I'm Marian!" I tell her.

For a moment, she just looks confused. Because, apparently, she has not spent every minute of the last week thinking about the cast announcement. Weird.

"Oh," she says. Finally. "Congratulations."

Even though she doesn't sound nearly enthusiastic enough, I let it slide. "Thanks."

Maddie clutches her hands together and fidgets with her thumbs. She always does that when she gets nervous. After a long pause, she clears her throat. I would never tell her, but right now she looks kind of sick. Gah. I hope she doesn't actually throw up or anything. "Did you . . . did you see my name on the list?"

I smile at her. "You're my mother."

"I'm your WHAT?" Maddie says. She almost drops the stack of books in her arms. I reach out to catch them, just in case.

"In the musical," I say slowly. "You're going to be Mrs. Paroo. It's a good part. Congratulations!"

Maddie runs a hand through her hair, and for a second I worry she's going to tear out a big chunk of it.

"I didn't want a good part!" she says. "I wanted a nothing part."

Over the last month, Maddie has said that about a bajillion times. But for some reason I can't really explain, I think she's lying. I'm almost sure of it.

"Well, you don't have a nothing part," I tell her. "Come on! We'll get to be in lots of scenes together. I'll help you through it. Super-swear."

Maddie blinks. She stares at me for way too long.

"Does Mrs. Paroo dance?" she asks.

I fidget with my hands. Obviously, Maddie is concerned about dancing. She has this thing called dyspra-something, and she's really clumsy. But is that a reason for her to not do anything ever? Seriously.

I shrug. "I don't think Mrs. Paroo dances a whole lot."

That may not be true. I don't know. But it's what Maddie wants to hear, so that's what I say.

Her shoulders lose just a tiny bit of their tension, and I mentally congratulate myself. "Okay. I guess I can do it."

That's something, at least.

"I'll help you learn the dance," I promise. "There are all sorts of tricks you can use to get better. I'll show you."

Maddie still looks doubtful, but she doesn't say anything. I grin as we walk to social studies together. Maddie definitely doesn't grin back, but fine. Maybe she just needs some time to get used to the whole idea.

We slide into our usual seats. I'm behind Kaitlyn, the

new girl from Seattle. She glances back at me with a bright smile.

"Chloe?" Maddie says. "Did you hear what I just said?"

Blinking, I turn back to her. "Uh, no?"

Maddie sighs, so quiet I barely notice. "Never mind."

CHAPTER SEVEN

Maddie

I don't talk to anyone after finishing up my audition. I can see Chloe, I can tell she wants to talk to me about something or other, but I flee the scene. That is one of my greatest talents, after all.

At least the afternoon is blissfully free of singing, dancing, and anything else related to the musical. Later I have my screenwriting elective, but first our cabin has free swim. I try my best to forget all about this morning's events as I slip off my T-shirt and flip-flops.

The moment I submerge myself into the pool, my entire body relaxes. This is why I love swimming. My issues with dyspraxia aren't really a problem in the water. Here, there is no danger of tripping, of falling, of humiliating myself in front of everyone. No one is watching me, waiting for me to mess up. I can just float on my back and remain undisturbed by the world.

I pull myself backward with grace I could never manage on solid ground. I close my eyes and allow the sun to wash over my skin.

PER-KLUMP.

The sting of chlorinated water slaps up against my face and shoulders. I sputter and spin out of my floating position. With gritted teeth, I open my eyes.

"Sorry!" this girl says. I think her name is Mara. Maybe I am being uncharitable, but she does not sound sorry.

"It's okay," I say. I give her a strained smile.

I start to swim away from Mara, into some undisturbed corner of the pool. But Mara starts talking again.

"How do you think auditions went?" she asks.

This was not a question I expected, and certainly not one that I want to discuss. I shrug a little.

"It was okay, I guess."

"How do you think I did?" she asks.

In all honesty, I don't remember a single thing about Mara's audition. But I know full well that saying so would not be polite.

"You were great."

She beams at me. "Thank you! That's what I thought, but it's hard to know for sure. You were pretty good, too."

"Uh, thanks?" I say. I probably should not have said it like a question, but I can't help but doubt any praise for my performance.

Besides, I didn't actually want to do well. A good audition means a good part, maybe even a lead part, and I absolutely cannot handle that. Maybe I should have performed badly on purpose. I would do just about anything to not get a good part.

I take a deep breath. In all likelihood, I have nothing to worry about. There are too many talented kids at Camp Rosewood, kids who actually want to perform, for me to get a major role. Besides, one of the leads is going to Chloe, just like always.

As I run through all the possibilities for what role I might get and how much potential for humiliation awaits, Mara continues talking. I barely pay attention to her, but one thing she says catches my attention.

"... onstage with Chloe," Mara says. "Wouldn't that be great?"

My face loses any trace of a smile. "What about Chloe?" I ask, hoping that my voice does not betray me. After all, I'm not supposed to care about Chloe, one way or the other.

"Well, she's going to be Elphaba. Duh!" Mara says.

Even Mara knows that Chloe is guaranteed the lead role.

"I want to be Galinda!" she continues. "So that we can perform together."

"Uh-huh," I say.

I can't bring myself to say anything more. Obviously, I can't tell Mara that performing with Chloe is not all it's cracked up to be, especially if her performance is anything less than absolutely perfect. I want to tell her, but I don't.

She probably wouldn't believe me if I tried.

"So, how about you? What role do you want?"

I gulp, and try to keep myself above water while I come up with an acceptable response.

"Nothing major," I say finally. "Just a small role. Hopefully one without too much dancing."

Despite the coolness of the water, my cheeks heat up. Why did I add that part about dancing? It does make me seem rather pathetic. Then again, Mara has seen The Video. She already knows all about my dancing woes.

As if to prove my point, Mara nods vigorously. "Of

course! I guess you wouldn't want a big part after . . . after everything that happened."

She is, of course, completely right. But there's just something about the way she says it that gives me an itch. Didn't I already tell her that I do not want to talk about this, ever? I guess she just forgot. Chloe sometimes forgot the things I told her, too.

I force myself to pause before answering. No matter how irritated I am, I don't want to show it. I should be nice and agreeable, and I'm pretty sure that snapping at another girl in a pool is not that. No matter how very much she deserves it.

"I'm really more of a screenwriter," I say in my most calm voice. "I'd much rather do that, but the program was canceled."

Mara's head bobs with a vigorous nod. "Of course. That makes sense. You seem like a screenwriter to me."

I should be happy to hear that I seem like a screenwriter. That is what I want, after all. But coming from Mara, it hardly feels like a compliment. Because I can't help but wonder. Why does she think I seem like a screenwriter? Am I not good enough to be a performer?

No, you're not, a nasty voice informs me. *Not talented enough, not graceful enough . . . and not thin enough.*

"By the way," Mara says. "I love your swimsuit. Sooo brave of you to wear it."

My attention returns to Mara. I try to tell myself she's just giving me a compliment, but something about it just annoys me. It's a pretty nice swimsuit, with a fun turquoise pattern that I love, but how am I brave for wearing it?

"Thanks," I mumble. I kind of hate myself for being so nice to her, but I don't know what else I can say.

"Of course!" Mara says. She hesitates for just a moment before continuing her blather. When she talks again, her voice is quieter and more serious. "I've been meaning to tell you something."

I know this isn't going anywhere good, but I don't know how to shut her up. I think of Chloe and her disdainful glare. Right now, I wish so much I could summon that myself.

"I used to be ten pounds heavier," Mara says. "Then I started eating different and exercising more. So maybe I can help you with the . . . you know."

I grind my teeth. The *you know* is my body—my body that is both too big and not enough.

If my moms were here, I know what they would say. People like Mara are wrong. *Empty-headed*, Mom would say. Small in a way that has nothing to do with body size or shape. But all of that feels very, very far away at the moment. I look around at the other kids. When we're all in our swimsuits, the difference between me and everyone else is more obvious than ever. I'm fat, fatter than pretty much every other kid here. And maybe I shouldn't mind, maybe that doesn't really matter, but it does. It matters.

"Excuse me," I tell Mara. "I have to go now."

I wish I could hide. But, of course, that is the one thing that I cannot do.

So I do the next-best thing. I rocket out of the pool and cover myself up with a towel as quickly as I can manage. As

if that will somehow make me smaller and more acceptable to the Maras of the world.

I think back to the auditions and the video and everything that happened last year. And I wish with all of my heart that Audrey casts me in a role so small that no one sees me.

I admit it. I mope around for a bit after my horrible conversation with Mara. But then I try to pull myself together. My screenwriting elective is before dinner, and I am not going to let Mara ruin that for me.

"Welcome!" Hannah says.

She smiles at the group of us—about twelve people huddled into the arts and crafts pavilion. It isn't quite what I imagined—the table in front of me is speckled with leftover glitter and bits of glue—but I smile back. This is why I came to camp, after all. Here, at last, I am in the right place. A place where I can write scenes instead of trying to perform them. Maybe this summer hasn't exactly followed the right script, but now I have a chance to correct it.

"If you're here, I don't need to give you a whole speech about how important screenwriters are," Hannah says. "You know that already. Most screenwriters aren't as famous as big-name actors, or even some directors. But without writers, there would be no movies, no TV, no theater. All the magic starts right here, with a blank page."

I straighten up in my stool, uncomfortable and too-small though it is. My brand-new purple notebook gleams in front of me. I can fill up those blank pages with anything I

want—superheroes, sorcerers, aliens. Some fantastical crea-
ture that's never been seen before, even. If only I can come
up with something.

I can. This is my thing. It has to be my thing.

". . . spark your creativity," Hannah says. I must have
missed something. She pulls out a battered black top hat and
starts to pass it around. "Now, you're going to pick a setting
for the movie you're going to write this summer."

Wait. We're going to pick the setting, a key element of
any screenplay, from a hat?

"Do we have to?" someone complains.

"Just keep an open mind and give it a try," Hannah says.
"Sometimes when you're given a set of constraints, your
creativity can really thrive."

Most of the other kids still appear doubtful, but one by
one they pick a piece of paper from the hat. Finally, it's my
turn. I chew on my cheek as I unfold the slip of paper.

London in the 1800s, it says in slanted handwriting.

A historical setting? I've never written anything like that
before, and I don't know if I really want to. But Hannah
said we should keep an open mind, so I guess I should.

She instructs us to spend the next fifteen minutes brain-
storming about our setting. I stare at the piece of paper,
willing it to give me some kind of brilliant idea. Nothing
much comes.

Three minutes into it, something starts to fall into place.
Even if the movie takes place in the past, it can still have
magic and superpowers. Yes! Maybe my main character is

actually a vampire? No, that's been done too many times. A werewolf? No, that has the exact same problem.

I want to do something fantastic, something that's never, ever been done before. I consider. There haven't really been many—or any—superhero movies with Jewish girls. I know there are Jewish superheroes in the Marvel comics, but none of the movies focus on them. I remember feeling really disappointed about it as a little kid. When I asked my moms about it, they said that I'd just need to write one myself. Well, now I can.

For this screenplay I can do something magic-y and Jewish. There were Jewish people in London during the 1800s. I know that much.

Problem is, I'm not exactly an expert in any of this. Still. My moms bought me a book about Jewish mythology for Hanukkah a few years ago, and I remember some of the stories. I think of a golem—a person created out of clay. In the book, all of the golems were boys. I guess girl golems and nonbinary golems don't exist, or at least no one has bothered to write a story about them. But maybe my story can be about a girl golem. That feels right to me.

A golem is kind of a superhero. At least, they have superstrength and speed or whatever. I'm not really clear on all the details, but it doesn't matter. I can make up whatever I want. That's the fun of screenwriting.

My golem girl will be strong. She will be brave. She will truly deserve to have her own movie, and possibly a sequel or two. (It never hurts to dream big, right?)

Just as I'm starting to write down possible names for my girl golem superhero, Hannah comes over. "Hey," she says. "What do you have?"

I start to describe the concept to her, and she nods. "That's a great start."

"It's just setting and character, though. That's not a story."

"Not yet," she agrees. "So let's figure out the story. What does this character want?"

I consider.

A golem is a person made out of clay. A person created by a Jewish wizard, or something. In the stories I know, even the people who make golems don't think their creations are real people. Golems are sort of like magical robots—never quite real enough, never quite good enough. A golem knows what it's like to be betrayed by a friend. A golem knows what it's like to have people laugh at you. A golem knows what it's like for some jerk to interrupt your afternoon just to inform you that your body isn't right. That *you* aren't right.

So, what does my golem want? I speak my answer out loud the moment it comes to me. "She wants respect," I say.

"Yes! Respect from who?"

"From . . . from the people who wronged her," I say. "She wants to show the world that she's good enough."

"That's great!"

As the pieces start falling together, I smile and grab my pen.

CHAPTER EIGHT

Chloe

I spend the rest of the day trying not to think about things. Namely, the musical and what part I'm going to get. And also Maddie and the way she so obviously avoided me today. Maybe she hates me even worse than I thought.

So I try to force myself into thinking about something else. Anything else, really. But somehow those two topics keep coming back to me. I can't even listen to music as a distraction, because music means the musical means worrying about casting.

Blech.

I try to be cool about it. While our cabin walks over to dinner, I oh-so-casually stroll up to Audrey.

"When are we going to find out about casting?" I ask at once.

Well, okay. Maybe I'm not so cool and casual.

Audrey flashes a close-mouthed smile. "Not long at all. I'll post the list tomorrow."

"When tomorrow?"

"Right before breakfast. I don't dawdle. We'll need all the time we can scrounge up to become performance ready."

Still smiling, Audrey points to a corkboard in front of the mess hall. Big bubble letters inform me that it is for ANNOUNCEMENTS.

Okay then. I check my watch. There are fifteen hours before I find out if I'm Elphaba. Sure, I'll theoretically be asleep for much of that time. But it still feels way too long.

I give Audrey my biggest and brightest grin. That usually works for grown-ups.

"So, what are you thinking?" I ask. "I can keep a secret."

"I am thinking that our evening activity is going to be awesome tonight," Audrey says. "It's going to be a trivia contest, all about the performing arts. You'll love it, I can promise you that."

Before I can stop myself, I make a face. So do not care.

"I am also thinking," Audrey continues, "that I am not going to tell you anything until tomorrow. Sorry, but that's how it goes."

Ugh, she is so not helpful. I mumble a goodbye and slink away.

The next morning, I force myself to get up early. I reach the dining hall a full fifteen minutes before everyone else. Aside from the cook, it's completely empty. So is the announcements board.

For the next ten minutes, I distract myself by running through vocal exercises. Then, I see Audrey's purple beret. My breaths become short and staccato.

I hang back and wait as she pins a piece of paper to the corkboard. Even though I want to run up and read it right away, I don't want to seem too desperate.

One second passes, then two. When I can't possibly stand waiting a moment longer, I rush forward to look.

There it is. The casting for Elphaba.

And it isn't me.

My mouth hangs open. Anger floods through my chest, and I almost don't bother reading the rest of the list. But I do. There's my name, right below Elphaba.

GALINDA——CHLOE WINTERS

So. I am going to be Galinda. The so-called good witch.

My teeth grind together. It's not a bad part, really. I know all the songs by heart, and they're fun. But even though Galinda is *a* lead part, she isn't *the* lead. Everyone knows that the most important character in *Wicked* is the wicked witch. I mean, duh.

I close my eyes and force myself to take deep breaths. After all, I know disappointment. I've been here before. When you do real Hollywood auditions, you pretty much expect not to get the part you want, ever.

But I thought this would be different. I don't mean to be arrogant or whatever, but I am so obviously the most talented person here.

How could you let this happen, Chloe? a voice asks. Cordelia's voice, of course. *You're supposed to get whatever you want.*

I tried! I argue back to the voice. *I really tried.*

Obviously not hard enough, fake Cordelia says.

The smart thing to do would be to shut up and stew in my misery for a while. But that's just not me. So I find Audrey. She's sitting at an empty table, reading through a thick stack of papers.

"Why, hello, Chloe," she says. As if she hadn't just ruined the next month of my life.

"Why am I not Elphaba?" I ask. Not very subtle, but this is no time for subtlety.

Audrey looks up from her papers and frowns at me.

"Galinda is a great, great part. Some people might say it's actually the most interesting role in the entire musical."

Some people. But definitely not me.

"Is it because I have red hair?" I ask. "Because I can totally wear a wig! Or dye my hair, even."

"Hair color had no impact on my decision. Chloe, I am an Asian American woman trying to make it in musical theater. I know what it's like to experience discrimination. So I don't do casting based on appearances—not now, not ever."

Her tone is gentle, but firm. I flush. Okay, maybe it was silly of me to accuse her of hair color discrimination or whatever. I know that's not a real thing, not like actual racism. But I still don't get it.

"Why then?" I ask. "Why didn't I get Elphaba?"

Audrey's lips pucker into a thin line. She sighs.

"The casting isn't a punishment, Chloe," she says. Her voice is strained. I have enough experience being fake nice to recognize when someone else is doing it. "Galinda is a terrific role, like I said. The entire musical really rests on her transformation. And the part calls for an actor with a higher vocal range, a true soprano. That's you. Elphaba's part is more suitable for Sasha. She's an alto. I can see your voices contrasting beautifully on the duets, once you put in the work."

The annoying part is that what she's saying actually makes sense. I choose to ignore it.

"I can do Elphaba's part. I have the vocal range."

88

"That may be true. But I think you can really learn a lot and thrive as Galinda."

With another tight smile, Audrey looks back to her papers. The message is clear: This conversation is over. And I'm not getting what I want.

Somehow—impossibly—I have failed.

As I eat breakfast and get myself mentally ready for rehearsal number one, a nagging thought keeps running through my mind. *I'm not good enough.* I don't know why, but I'm not. If I were really talented, then I'd be Elphaba, wouldn't I? Audrey can talk all she likes about how Galinda is a great role and how I'm a soprano or whatever. Doesn't matter. I know the truth.

I arrive at rehearsal early. To distract myself, I take out my headphones and program my playlist to shuffle. But the very first song that comes up is "No One Mourns The Wicked." With gritted teeth, I yank my headphones out. I don't know why, but the universe is out for me today.

Just as I'm about to start on some vocal exercises, someone else arrives. Maddie.

For a long moment, neither of us says anything. I think maybe I can get away with not talking to her. But then Maddie clears her throat.

"Congratulations," she says, voice flat. "You must be happy."

"Not really," I say. Because I just can't help myself, I guess.

Maddie raises an eyebrow. "But . . . you're one of the leads. How are you not happy?"

Even Maddie doesn't get it. She knows Cordelia, she's seen how Cordelia works, and still she doesn't get it. An itch works its way through my skin.

"I wanted to be Elphaba," I explain. I mean, hello, this seems kind of obvious, but okay. Maybe Maddie just needs it explained to her.

Maddie scrunches her forehead. I don't know what that means. Lately her faces have been a total mystery to me.

"So," she says after a long pause. "You're mad that you didn't get exactly what you wanted."

My cheeks become hot and uncomfortable. When she puts it that way, I sound like I'm spoiled or something. But I'm totally not!

Am I?

No, no, that's ridiculous. I just want what I want. And I want to make my mother happy. Who can possibly blame me for that?

"I just thought that my performance was good enough for Elphaba," I say, crossing my arms. "So I'm a little disappointed. That's all."

"Uh-huh."

After that, Maddie doesn't say anything. Just purses her lips and walks away. Ugh, what is up with her? Before, she always listened when I complained about stuff. No matter how small or silly the thing. Now, it's like everything I say just makes her hate me even more.

Suddenly, a thought pops into my mind. I remember the sneer on her lips as she talked to me. Her eye roll. Is she jealous of me or something?

I've wondered about this once or twice before, but I've always discarded the idea. Why would Maddie be jealous of me when she knows what Cordelia is like? Like I wouldn't rather have her moms a thousand times over!

Before, I always managed to convince myself that I was just imagining things. Now? I'm not so sure.

Maddie

The auditorium chairs are completely empty, but that does not comfort me. In less than two months, every single seat will have a person in it to watch me fail spectacularly.

Maybe the worst part is, I hate *The Music Man*. Truly, *hate* is not a strong enough word. I loathe *The Music Man*. I positively despise it.

More than anything else, I hate my part. Chloe can blabber on about how Mrs. Paroo is an important part and I'm a good singer and all her other lies, but I know the real reason why I got the part. Who better than the fat girl to play the ridiculous mother character?

I don't say this to Chloe. She would only protest that I'm wrong, and I know I'm not. There are some things that Chloe—thin, perfect, graceful Chloe—can never understand. Besides, it's not as though Chloe even cares all that much about my problems. She got exactly what she wanted: the lead role and rides home from rehearsals. Everything works out perfectly for Chloe Winters, just like it always does.

Meanwhile, I am suffering through the nightmare that is dancing. Chloe promised me that I wouldn't have to dance much, but Ms. W didn't get that memo. She seems to think that everyone in the cast should be able to kick and twirl and jump on cue. I've thought about trying to explain to her that I just can't, that I have dyspraxia. But

I've tried this before with teachers. Last year I tried talking to my gym teacher about dyspraxia. She said "sure," but then took points off my grade when I couldn't finish the obstacle course. If Ms. W is like that, why should I even bother telling her anything?

So here I am, practicing the opening number with everyone else.

All around me, people break into song. "You really ought to give Iowa a try!"

I know the words, and I should be singing them, too. But I absolutely cannot force my mouth to sing and my feet to step-step-step-turn at the same time. I can't even manage to force my feet left when they need to go left and right when they need to go right. I should have a fifty-fifty chance of getting it right, but somehow I never do.

At least *The Music Man* has destroyed my silly dream about becoming a star. Now I know beyond a shadow of a doubt that it can never, ever happen. If I can get through the show without injuring myself, I will count that as a victory. I should not hope for anything more. It's better for me to be a screenwriter, safely tucked away backstage.

"Provided you are contrary!" the group sings, finishing off the song.

I yank my arms up for one final pose, hoping that's actually the right choreography. It's all so hard to remember.

To my eternal relief, Ms. W stops the music and calls for a break. I instinctively search for Chloe. We've found a little nook backstage where we can hang out when we don't have to rehearse.

She smiles widely, and I try to return it. In all honesty, whenever I see her I can't help but resent her for all of my *Music Man* misery. She doesn't get it.

I've explained my dyspraxia to Chloe before, of course. But sometimes . . . sometimes she acts like that evil gym teacher from last year. Maybe she'll say the right things, but she doesn't really believe me when I say I can't do something. Instead, she insists that I can do the thing if I just try hard enough. As though I actually enjoy tripping over my feet all the time! Which, for the record, I do not.

"You just have to watch your hands," Chloe tells me. "When you dance."

"What?"

When I dance, I can't even begin to think about my hands. My feet keep me busy enough.

"It's a way to tell the difference between left and right. Your left hand makes the letter *L*, see?"

She holds up her left hand to demonstrate, and I follow. She's right. My thumb forms the bottom of the L, holding up the rest of my fingers.

"So if you just follow the L hand, you know which way you're going," Chloe says.

It's a useful trick. Maybe I won't ever be a great dancer, but with a little luck and a lot of work, I can at least avoid embarrassing myself. At least, I hope so.

"Thanks," I say.

Chloe flashes another smile. "Sure. I learned that when we had to do action sequences on the TV show. That

choreo was way trickier than anything Ms. W comes up with."

I know she doesn't mean to brag, exactly, but her explanation is bragging. Sometimes I wonder if Chloe even knows she's doing it, but how can she not? I press my lips together and nod.

Ms. W calls us back to rehearsal, and my pulse skitters. Luckily, the next scene we rehearse does not include Mrs. Paroo. As I watch the other kids perform, I wonder if any of them feel like me. Like they don't belong here at all. In all honesty, I'd quit if it weren't for the fact that I would look completely pathetic.

"Maddie!" Ms. W calls a mere twenty minutes later. "We need you center stage."

I suppress a sigh and shuffle back to the stage, where Carlos, a.k.a. Harold Hill, is waiting for me. When I realize which scene we're practicing, I stifle a groan. I try not to show my horror as I take up my place.

The music starts up, and Carlos sings "Gary, Indiana." I join him right on cue, and I do okay. The song itself isn't difficult. I have five lines, and all of them are firmly committed to my memory.

I can do this. I can be Mrs. Paroo.

But then, of course, we have to dance.

Carlos spins through his part of the song. While he isn't a great dancer, he more or less gets all the steps. Then he holds out a hand for me. I grab it and spin into his arms, then out. That's one part of the dance down.

95

Now, we are supposed to do a leg kick together. I take a deep breath and prepare myself.

My right leg takes off and kicks Carlos squarely in his skinny chest. He topples over. I realize, too late, that I was supposed to kick with my left leg.

I yelp. "I am so sorry," I tell him. I repeat it at least three times.

Carlos picks himself up from the wooden stage, wincing ever so slightly. "It's okay, Maddie. I signed up for this."

Luckily for me, Carlos is super nice. I'm not sure how many other boys would be so calm about being kicked in the chest. Still, I can't help but notice that he wobbles a bit on his feet after my mess-up.

Ms. W suggests moving on to another scene. Thankfully, it does not include me. I race toward our backstage nook the moment she's done speaking.

Chloe is there, of course. "The trick with the hand didn't work, I guess? Sorry."

"No. It didn't."

I don't say anything else to Chloe. I just stare into space, wondering how I can possibly make it through the next few months.

Chloe

Normally I love rehearsal. But today is different.

It's not like I'm worried about my performance or anything. Of course not. But there's still a problem. A seriously major problem.

I don't want to kiss Carlos. And I especially don't want to kiss Carlos in front of a bajillion people. Or at least all the kids in the musical.

We haven't rehearsed the whole scene yet. But Ms. W said we need to practice The Kiss, and she strongly implied it would be today. So here I am, waiting backstage. Right now, a bunch of boys are practicing the "Lida Rose" number. Normally I enjoy the song, but not now. And it's not just because at least half the singers have no sense of pitch. No, the real problem is the thoughts flitting through my mind. Making my stomach hurt.

"Chloe," Maddie says from her spot next to me. "You okay?"

I open my mouth. Really, I want to tell her. About kissing Carlos, about the weird feelings I've been having, about . . . everything, really. Even if I don't 100 percent know what "everything" even is. Maddie is a good friend—the best, really—and if anyone will understand all of the weirdness I'm feeling, it's her. But I can't bring myself to tell her about it. I don't know why. Maybe I'm just a coward like that.

"I'm fine," I tell her.

My hands clench together. I wonder if maybe Maddie can tell that I'm not fine. Aren't, like, psychic best friend powers a thing?

She looks at me for a long time. Then shrugs. "Okay."

I grind my teeth.

"Lida Rose" wraps up, thankfully for my ears. Unthankfully, however, Ms. W calls me to the stage. Carlos is already there, hopping from one foot to another. I've never seen him so nervous. Not even when he has to dance with Maddie.

We don't look at each other.

"I know this is a little awkward," Ms. W says. "That's why we're going to get all of the awkwardness out of the way now and not in front of the audience."

I nod. Makes perfect sense. But that doesn't mean I actually want to do this. Still, Chloe Winters is nothing if not an actor, and a darn good one. So I'll do it. I lift my head and turn my gaze toward Carlos. He gives me a small grin.

"If it helps, I don't like you," he says. "I mean, I do like you as a friend. But not like *that*."

"I don't like you like *that*, either," I say. So true.

Carlos widens his smile. "Cool. I, uh, didn't want that to come out the wrong way. Just so you know, I'm gay. So I don't really like girls at all."

I nod. For some reason, my throat dries up. I want to say something, but I can't quite get the words out. Gah. I hope Carlos doesn't think I mind that he's gay. Because I totally don't. Actually, I'd like to ask him how he figured it all out.

And maybe also some other things. But now is so not the time for that.

Ms. W claps her hands together. "You two are great actors. I know you can do this. So I'd like you to kiss when I count to three, okay?"

We glance at each other and nod.

"One . . ."

I take a deep breath. Maybe Carlos and I don't like each other *like that*, but this is still super awkward.

"Two . . ."

He leans forward. I lean forward.

"Three . . ."

Our lips touch for like two seconds, then we pull apart. His lips are kind of moist. Blech. I resist the urge to wipe my mouth.

"Excellent!" Ms. W says. "Do it like that during the performance, and it will be just fine."

I sigh with relief. Awkwardness over, at least for now. Now comes the easy part: our duet.

When I sing, I forget about the fact that Carlos is a slightly geeky boy who does not like girls. I forget that Maddie sort of has a point about how this musical is sexist. I even forget that I'm me. He's Harold Hill, and I'm Marian Paroo, and we are standing on a bridge as we finally confess our feelings for each other. And we're doing it through song, the best and truest way to say anything.

". . . till there was you," we finish together.

As the final note fades, the specialness of the moment ends. Suddenly I have to be Chloe again. I shake myself.

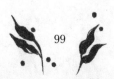

Ms. W instructs Carlos and me to stand a little closer together, but gives us a thumbs-up. We're done rehearsing, at least for now.

I slink off to my and Maddie's hideout. Unfortunately, it's been invaded. Maddie sits in her usual spot, flipping through a book. But she isn't alone. A few of the other girls in the musical have, apparently, discovered us. I guess they want to talk to me. I don't want to talk with them, but no one's given me a choice.

"Chloe!" this one girl Michelle says. She plays the mayor's wife. The character is completely ridiculous, and it suits Michelle perfectly.

"Yeah?" I say.

Michelle and her two friends giggle. Ugh, why are they here? Do they not understand the concept of personal space?

I glance toward Maddie, hoping that she'll somehow figure out a way to save me from this conversation. But she's still reading her book—or pretending to read, probably. I'm on my own.

"So . . . what was it like?" one of Michelle's friends asks. I can't be bothered to remember her name.

"What was what like?" I cross my arms over my chest.

"Duh! Kissing Carlos."

I shrug. "Fine."

Maybe not the most detailed explanation, but this is totally not their business.

"That's it?" Michelle asks.

"Yeah. We're actors."

Seriously, I know that Michelle is pretty ignorant, but

after two months of rehearsals I would expect that even she'd understand the whole acting thing.

"But . . . it's Carlos! He's so cute," says Whatever Her Name.

I resist the urge to roll my eyes. Carlos isn't interested in any of these girls. But I don't have the right to tell them about his sexuality.

"I am an actor. I don't have to like Carlos romantically to perform with him," I say.

Michelle and the others frown at that.

"So, if you don't like Carlos, who do you like?"

I immediately think of Kaitlyn from social studies class . . . but I can't tell them that. Cordelia's voice from forever ago echoes in my head. *People might think you're a lesbian. That's not the image we want to project.*

"No one," I say at once. "I don't really like anyone."

Including you, I add silently.

They get bored with this conversation, I guess, because they go away. Maddie looks up from her book.

"Awkward," she says.

"Yeah."

Not like she did anything to save me from the awkwardness. But I don't say it, because maybe that wouldn't be fair. Maddie doesn't like talking to people she doesn't know. And, unlike me, she can't even fake it.

I look around. We're alone. Or at least alone-ish. I can talk to her now, maybe.

I want to talk to her. About how it isn't just Carlos— I don't like any boy, and is that weird?

101

If anyone will understand, it's *Maddie*. Even though I don't exactly know what I should call myself, I know she'll accept me. One of her moms is bisexual, and the other is a lesbian.

Maddie, I think maybe I like girls.

I want to tell her. But I don't.

CHAPTER NINE

Maddie

NOW: JULY

Somehow, I get through the first few days of *Wicked* rehearsals. I do not enjoy them, but at the very least I manage to avoid utter humiliation. Always, I make a special effort to avoid Chloe. It helps that she spends most of her time rehearsing with her fellow leads, while I am a lowly side character. My character's name is Vanessa. She is a student at Shiz, the magic school that Elphaba and Galinda and all the rest of them attend. I don't remember her from the actual musical, but Audrey revised it so that more kids have lines. I guess she wants everyone to feel important. Personally, I would rather be a tree. Or a rock, which is even less important than a tree.

At least I have my screenplay to occupy my mind. In every spare moment, I've been scribbling in my notebook— bits of dialogue and notes for future scenes, mostly. Little by little, the scenes are becoming more vivid. The movie begins when my golem character, who I have named Adina, wakes up in the streets of London. She wanders around, confused. One boy throws rocks, but Adina's clay skin protects her. Something else needs to happen, I know, but I can't quite figure out what. Maybe I need to write in another character, someone who can provide banter and contrast and all of that.

Should I give Adina a friend? Do golems have friends?

Right now, there isn't time to figure it out. Rehearsal begins in ten minutes. My character only has a few lines, but I will be in three different dance numbers. Even the idea of having to dance onstage makes my skin crawl and my pulse race.

I've thought about talking to Audrey. I could tell her about my dyspraxia and all of the problems that come with it. I could beg her to let me not dance, or at least cut out a number or two. But I don't.

I guess I *can't*, for whatever stupid reason. Maybe Audrey should have cast me as the cowardly lion instead.

Today, when I arrive in the barn, the chairs are arranged differently—in a circle, not rows. I gulp. Just as I am sort of getting used to being in the musical, we're doing something new?

Audrey stands on one of the chairs and calls everyone to attention. Even after nearly a week at camp, it still amazes me how the ridiculously loud theater kids shut up when she gives the order.

"Today, we won't be venturing into the land of Oz. At least, not at first," she says.

Whispers break out among the crowd. Chloe, I notice, does not look happy.

"Of course, we still need to hone our skills as performers. Today, we are going to work on our ability to think quickly and improvise on the spot," Audrey explains.

I fidget with my hands. While I don't know what Audrey has planned, exactly, her words are not comforting.

Audrey rolls her hands in a motion that I think is supposed to look like a drum roll. "So! We are going to be playing that game you all know and love . . . improv freeze tag!"

Cheers erupt all around me, but I stay completely still. I don't know what improv freeze tag is, but I don't think I am going to like it.

As Audrey goes over the rules, the knot in my stomach grows bigger and bigger. She explains that two kids will act out a scene that they make up on the spot. Then, someone will replace one of the actors, and they will start an entirely new scene. No scripts, no directions.

"Just your brains and bodies!" Audrey says. "And some props, if you feel so inspired."

She points to a box at the center of the circle. Clenching my fists, I try my best not to panic.

I think about Adina. She would be able to handle a bit of stress, wouldn't she? I should be able to do it, too, even if I'm not made of clay.

So I fight back worries about the impending disaster and watch as improv freeze tag begins. Two kids act out a scene of contestants sabotaging each other at a baking competition. Another pair pretends to be penguin siblings.

Then Audrey points at me. "You're up, Maddie!"

I gulp.

My scene partner is a boy named Calvin. At least, I think that's what his name is. Since I am the new actor, I should begin the scene. But I have absolutely no ideas.

"Just act out the first thing that comes into your mind!" Audrey says.

The first thing that comes into my mind is a desire to run out of the room. Obviously, I can't do that. The second thing that comes into my mind is that maybe I can be an alien. I certainly feel like one at the moment.

"Greetings to you!" I say to maybe-Calvin. "I have just arrived from the planet Thort. I am completing a mission on behalf of my people, the Thortanki Empire. I would like to be informed about recreational activities here in the land of humans."

Probably-Calvin smiles at me, and I relax ever so slightly. "You're an alien? Cool! Can I take a video with you for You-Tube?"

From there, we act out a slightly ridiculous scene in which my human guide introduces alien-me to fast food. When I start munching on imaginary fries, Audrey orders us to freeze.

"Good job, Chris," she says. Okay, so he's not Calvin. "You're out for now."

I know what comes next. Audrey is going to pick a new scene partner for me. I mentally cross my fingers, hoping it isn't Chloe. Of course, it is. Chloe hops up to the stage and gives me a tentative smile. I do not return it.

"Begin scene!" Audrey announces.

Chloe doesn't even hesitate. She looks at me and lets out a blood-curdling shriek. "Watch out, watch out! You're going to crash the plane!"

A plane crash? That's what she decided to do? Well, fine. I can run with this. I know how to deal with Chloe, after all.

"Don't distract me!" I snap at her. "I'm trying to navigate . . . oh. Oh no! We're falling!"

Chloe starts flailing around onstage before I'm even done speaking. "We're going to die! We're going to die."

While she acts out crashing the plane onto a deserted island, I start rummaging through the prop box. My hand brushes up against a plastic snake and I smile. I pull it out and swing it around like a whip. I am careful to avoid actually hitting Chloe.

"This island is infested!" I cry. "The snakes . . . they're . . . they're everywhere!"

Chloe stares at the snake and twists her face into disgust. I don't think she's acting, at least, not entirely. Chloe has always been squeamish about bugs and reptiles, even fake ones. Maybe it's mean, but I give myself a figurative pat on the back.

Then Chloe draws herself up. "We have to fight it! Here, let me grab my knife."

To me, the sudden addition of a knife feels a little like cheating, but I play along as she makes a big show of attacking the snake. "Look! There's another one!" I cry. "We'll never survive."

Chloe grins dangerously. "No snake stands a chance against me."

Maybe it's ridiculous, but I can't help but resent the way Chloe has played the scene. Even here, in this completely made-up skit, she has to make herself the big hero. I'm the sidekick, just like always.

Unless, of course, I do something about it.

Before I can think too hard about what I am doing, I jab an accusing finger toward Chloe.

"You know," I say. "It's totally your fault that we crashed the plane in the first place!"

Huh? What possessed me to say that?

"What?" Chloe says, echoing my thoughts. She sounds genuinely confused.

That makes two of us, really, but I press on.

"I was the pilot, I should have been the one in charge, but you kept telling me what to do and then we . . ."

"I didn't do anything to you!" Chloe says. She sounds like real-Chloe, not actor-Chloe.

I force myself to stand up a little bit straighter. "Yes, you did! And now we're stuck on this awful island with the people-eating snakes forever."

"Don't you think you're being a little unfair?" Chloe says, using the same high-pitched voice she always slips into when she gets irritated. "You didn't even tell me you were having problems!"

I ignore her. "Now thanks to you we're here, and it's terrible, and soon we'll probably be forced to eat each other, and . . ."

"Okay!" Audrey says. "Nice job, actors. It got a little clichéd at parts, but you really showed creativity with that cannibalism part, Maddie. Now you're out."

I blink. Part of me had forgotten that we were acting at all. But now it's over, thank goodness it's over.

In my rush back to my seat, I trip over my own foot and splay out over the floor.

"Let me help!" Chloe says. She offers me a hand.

I do not take it. I lift myself up from the floor all by myself.

"I don't need you," I tell Chloe.

Chloe stares at me coldly. "Fine. Be that way. I guess I won't bother with you the next time you fall. Which will probably be in, like, ten minutes, if I know anything about you."

The background soundtrack erupts with a few snickers. As I slink back to my seat, I feel like I really did just survive a plane crash.

Later, when the improv exercise is over, I volunteer to return the prop box to the closet. I stare at the snake, thinking of Chloe's reaction when she saw it. Thinking about how awful and humiliating it was to fall in front of everyone, yet again. And I think about my screenplay, the one thing here that's totally and completely mine.

Adina wants respect, yes . . . but how will she get it? How can she, in a world that mocks her at every turn?

All at once, I know what needs to happen. Adina will make a friend, but that friend doesn't really care about her. The new friend—let's call her Eunice—is going to humiliate Adina. I don't quite know how this happens. Maybe Eunice pushes Adina off a bridge or something. And then? Then Adina is going to seek her revenge.

Of course, if I want to write this and have it seem believable, I'll need to do a little firsthand research. I need to understand what it means to seek revenge if I want to write this scene and have it all seem real.

I grab the snake and stuff it into my bag.

CHAPTER TEN

Chloe

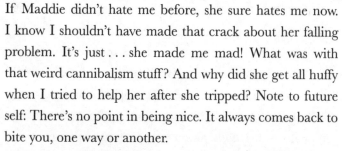

If Maddie didn't hate me before, she sure hates me now. I know I shouldn't have made that crack about her falling problem. It's just . . . she made me mad! What was with that weird cannibalism stuff? And why did she get all huffy when I tried to help her after she tripped? Note to future self: There's no point in being nice. It always comes back to bite you, one way or another.

The morning after the improv disaster, I wake up to a snake prop in my bed. I manage to stop myself from screaming. But it's a struggle. I toss the thing on Maddie's bed. "Hilarious," I say in my frostiest voice.

She flushes and I walk away. I should arrange for payback, probably. If I can think of the right thing. I file the thought away for future consideration, but I don't dwell on it. My top priority needs to be *Wicked*.

All things considered, I've done a pretty spectacular job during the first week of rehearsals. I already have all the songs memorized, obviously, and I'm doing pretty good on learning my spoken lines. I perform the choreography well. I even manage to hide my feelings about having the wrong role.

But something just feels off. For a while, I can't pinpoint the problem. Then it hits me. I spend hours with the same people every day, but I don't have a single friend. And I'm starting to realize that I sort of want one.

There must be a way to fix that. At today's lunch, I decide. I am going to find a new friend today. How hard could it be, really?

After I fill up my tray, I look around at the mess hall and consider the friend options.

The Shakespeare kids and the musical kids sit on different sides of the mess hall. I consider trying to make friends with one of the Shakespeare kids, but that won't solve my problem. And anyway, they're probably super annoying. So I look at the musical side of the room.

Maddie is seated at the nearest table, so that one is definitely out. The next one over has Mara, which is also a big nope. Ugh, maybe I should forget about this. I can find a friend some other time. Probably.

Just as I'm about to wander over to a mostly empty table in the corner, I notice a familiar head of dark, curly hair. Sasha walks toward me with her own lunch tray in hand. She smiles. (Is she smiling at me? Am I smiling back? I should smile back, right?)

I can see her lips start to make words, but I can't make them out with all the noise. I wish everyone else would just go away. And also, she is wearing the prettiest yellow sundress and . . .

My hand slips. The tray falls to the ground with a faint rattle. Minestrone soup splashes over my chest, scalding my skin.

I yelp. I cannot believe I dropped my lunch tray. In front of *Sasha*.

Everyone stares at me. Mara races over and offers to help, but I shoo her away. When Sasha offers me napkins, I accept.

"I'm okay," I keep saying. "Really."

Sasha doesn't say anything, but she does help me scoop up the now ruined food. When we're done, she smiles at me. "I'll save you a seat," she says.

My heart skitters. For some stupid reason.

For the next minute, I do my best to pick out the beans that have fallen on top of my boobs without actually undressing in front of everyone. So much yuck. Eventually, I manage to complete the bean removal.

As I get myself a new tray of food, it occurs to me that dropping things is really freaking inconvenient on top of all the embarrassment. Poor Maddie. She drops things at least three times a week. Maybe I should be nicer to her about it. I think back to my smart remark from a few days ago and wince.

Too late to do anything about it. I shake myself and walk over to Sasha's table.

"Uh, hi," I say. "Um. Thanks for inviting me. To, you know. Eat with you."

Blech, why am I acting like this? What is it about Sasha that makes my thoughts turn so sluggish? It's no wonder I dropped my tray in front of her.

She shrugs. "No problem. Actually, I've been meaning to talk with you."

My stupid heart picks up its pace again. "You . . . you have?"

"Yeah." Sasha twists her fingers. "I feel like things have been a little weird between us."

"Weird how?" I ask. Gah, I hate the way my voice squeaks. But she's seriously making me nervous. I mean, she can't possibly know all the thoughts I've been having, right?

Sasha stares at her fork. "Well, I know you really wanted to be Elphaba. So I thought maybe you were mad at me."

Oh. She thinks this is about the casting. Well, that's good. I guess.

"I'm not mad at you," I say honestly.

"But you are jealous?"

"Maybe a little," I admit. "But I can get over it. I don't want things to be weird between us."

I mean everything that I say. I really do want to have a good relationship with Sasha. I want that a whole lot.

"Excellent," Sasha says. "I don't want things to be weird between us, either."

For a moment, I forget about the fact that I have soup stains running down my shirt. I smile extra widely. Sasha raises an eyebrow, but she gives me that dazzling smile of hers.

"I'm glad we had this talk." She pauses. "You know, you're not nearly as scary as you seem at first."

My smile freezes in place. "Me? I'm scary?"

"Let's see. You're famous, beautiful, and, oh yeah, you know how to give a deathly glare." Sasha ticks off the points on her fingers. "Yeah, I'd say you're kind of scary. But now

that we're friends, I don't think that glare is going to work on me anymore."

She . . . she thinks I'm beautiful? Wow.

It doesn't mean anything. Girls say that sometimes. Besides, I am objectively attractive. Everyone knows that.

As Sasha continues staring at me, I realize I need to say something else. "We're . . . uh, we're friends now?"

I hate the uncertain crack in my voice. Chloe Winters is confident, always. Except when I'm not.

"Yeah, we're friends! Unless you don't want to be, of course."

"Yes! I mean . . . yes, I want to be friends."

Way to go, Chloe. There goes any chance she might still think of me as cool.

"We are officially friends," Sasha says.

Then she smiles at me again and I almost drop my fork.

Our afternoon rehearsal is not great. I mean, I didn't expect the kids here to perform at a professional level. Obviously. But still. Everyone else being not good disappoints me. Even Sasha is a little out of tune in one of our duets.

"Time for a break, crew," Audrey announces.

I frown. If you count lunch, we've already had four breaks today. I don't see a need for break number five. Not that anyone asked me.

Also, now that Sasha and I are friends I should probably spend time with her during break. Which would be good. Except . . . what if I say something stupid? Too much risk. Way, way too much.

Maybe I can pretend to be busy. I take a gulp from my

114

water bottle. Just as I'm about to slip on my headphones, the universal signal for don't-bother-me-thanks-and-bye, Mara approaches me. A big fake smile is planted on her face.

"Congratulations!" she tells me. Definitely a fake smile, and not even a good one.

I keep my own face neutral. It's an amazing feat of acting prowess, if I do say so myself. "Congratulations for what?"

"For getting Galinda! Really, I'd stab someone for a part that good. Non-fatally, of course."

All my instincts about this girl were 200 percent correct. I search for a convenient excuse to flee.

"All roles are important," I lie. "I'm just glad I get a chance to perform."

Yeah, that's total dog doo-doo.

"Uh-huh," Mara says. She doesn't believe that, either. "Actually, I wanted to talk to you about that."

Of course she would have some kind of not-so-hidden agenda. I sigh. "Yeah?"

"My part doesn't give me enough to do. Audrey isn't making use of all my talents! Just watch."

With that, she clutches her hand dramatically toward her chest. "Elphaba!" she cries. "Why can't you be calm for once?"

It's one of Galinda's lines from the show. I deliver it better, of course.

Mara straightens her body and looks at me with expectant eyes. "Well? What do you think?"

I shrug. Seriously, what am I supposed to say to her?

"You're . . . good."

I don't mean it, but I can't exactly say anything else.

Since Mara is, well, Mara, she beams like I just told her she won the Tony. "Oh my gosh, thank you, thank you! Can you tell that to Audrey?"

This time, I can't stop the frown that springs up on my face. "Why? What's that supposed to do?"

"So she can give me a better part!" Mara says in a "duh" voice.

I sigh. Right now, I just want to bury my head in my hands and walk away. But Mara likes me, for some reason, and walking away from someone who likes me isn't a Chloe Winters thing to do.

"I'm not in charge. I can't make Audrey do anything," I say.

If I made the casting decisions, I would have cast myself as the number-one lead. Duh. But I don't say that.

"Audrey will listen to you," Mara says.

"I really don't think so."

It's the truest thing I've said to her in this whole ridiculous conversation.

The fake smile that had been so firmly attached to Mara's face vanishes in all of one second. "You know, you're not really that great."

"Excuse me?" I say. I don't bother keeping the edge out of my voice.

"I said, you're not really that great. Sure, you can sing a little, but your acting sucks. Audrey only gave you a good part because you're famous."

116

She says *famous* like an insult. As if she hadn't sought me out for that exact reason.

"I'm sorry you feel that way," I tell her. It's a pretty darn nice response, given everything.

"Oh, you don't need to put on your nice act with me."

Heat prickles underneath my skin. "Excellent," I say. "In that case I can tell you that the real reason you don't have a good part is because you are not, nor will you ever be, a real actor."

Maybe that was too mean. I know. But she was mean first!

Mara glares at me. "At least I still have a chance at a real career," she says. "You, on the other hand, will be doing period commercials forever. Or maybe they'll upgrade you to diarrhea."

It's a pretty good shot. Even I can admit that. Before I can come up with a counter, Mara whooshes away, denying me the chance to get in the last word. It's super annoying.

I take another gulp of water and try to forget about the whole thing. Yeah, Mara is awful. But what can she really do to me? I try to shove all thoughts of her out of my head.

I need to do something, anything. I need to get my mind off Mara and her annoying-ness. Not to mention all the weird feelings I've been having. I remember Maddie and her stupid snake prank.

Time for some payback.

Maddie

With less than ten minutes before showtime, the backstage area is in sheer chaos. Between people talking too loudly and a group of boys practicing "Lida Rose," my attention keeps flickering from place to place.

Focus, I chant to myself. Just focus on me.

Unfortunately, me isn't doing particularly well at the moment. Between my too-tight costume and my nerves, it takes all of my energy to breathe normally.

Why did I ever allow Chloe to talk me into this?

But I did, and now I'm standing backstage trying to ignore the itchiness creeping all over my skin. The sweat soaking through my armpits.

I look at myself in the mirror and make a face at my reflection. I wish I didn't have to wear this green lacy monster of a costume. Apart from the fact that it's the most hideous thing I've ever worn, the woman who made it annoyed me. While she took my measurements, she tut-tutted about how much fabric she needed to use and didn't I know that I should eat less cake. Flames erupted in my cheeks while I tried to hold in my stomach as much as I could, hoping to make myself just a little bit smaller. Now the dress presses in on my body, smooshing my belly and the boobs that sprang from my chest way too quickly these past few months.

Sometimes—not all of the time, but sometimes—I wish I was just *less*. Less big, less round, less clunky. More like Chloe, who I'm sure has never been told to eat less cake.

The thoughts threaten to suffocate me. I close my eyes and try to push past it with a gulp of the raspberry lemonade Sandra made for me. At least my throat won't be dry when it's time for me to sing.

Chewing my lip, I glance over at Chloe. She, of course, looks entirely put together. Almost bored, really. If not for her beautiful blue dress, I would think she's sitting in math class, just waiting for our teacher to go over problem seven.

Right now, I cannot help but resent her, just a little bit.

"How are you like that?" I ask before I can think better of it.

She frowns at me. "Like what?"

Of course Chloe doesn't understand, not even a little. "Never mind," I say.

It's pointless even to hope that Chloe could understand anything I'm feeling right now.

But then she takes me by surprise.

"Maddie. I wanted to thank you."

The words sound strange coming out of Chloe's mouth.

"For what?" I ask.

"For doing all this. I know you didn't want to, but you did it for me."

I nod. Hearing her acknowledge that out loud makes my shoulders feel lighter. The knots in my chest still flutter, but it is something.

119

"You're very welcome," I say.

Although I thought that would be the end of this conversation, it isn't.

"If you have a . . . problem . . . onstage . . ." Chloe begins. "And I'm not saying anything bad will happen! I think you'll be great. You should be more confident in yourself."

I raise an eyebrow. "But if I do have a problem?"

"Then I'm here for you. Always."

She offers me a hand, and I squeeze it.

"Thanks," I say quietly.

Then, Ms. W's voice rings through the backstage area.

"Okay, team! We're on in five minutes."

I gulp.

I make my entrance. Even though I don't do much in the first scene, my heartbeat races faster than I ever thought possible. Part of it is nerves, yes, but there's also something else. Something that feels an awful lot like excitement.

I am really doing this. I am onstage performing. And maybe I'm not a star, exactly, but my role is an important one.

Somehow, I get through the first number, even the dancing parts. Maybe I don't totally nail all of Ms. W's choreography, but I stand in the back, so I don't think anyone will notice my less-than-graceful steps.

Then I get to act for real. The part of Mrs. Paroo is not exactly deep, but I think I nail it. I nag Chloe-as-Marian about finding a husband. I fuss over my "son," played by a

tall boy who is actually a year older than me. I don't even have to think about my lines consciously. They just come to me.

I am so focused on performing that I barely notice when the big moment arrives. My song and dance with Carlos. The whole thing happens in front of a wheelbarrow prop.

Before the number begins, I draw in a deep breath and give myself a pep talk. I did everything else, and I did it well. Surely I can do this, too.

"Gary, Indiana, let me say it once again . . ." Carlos sings.

I sing it back, every word and note as it should be.

I am really doing this.

Then . . . then it is time to dance. I draw in a deep breath.

Twirl, spin, no problem.

Kick left, yes.

Kick right, a little low but that's okay.

All the hard parts of the dance are over. I am really doing this. I've *done* it.

Now I just need to strut over to the wheelbarrow and strike my final pose. Easy-peasy, as Mom would say.

I lift one foot, then the other. And I trip.

It's only a minor stumble, really, but the mistake flusters me just the same. I know what I'm supposed to do, where I should position my arms, but my feet have completely escaped my control. They jerk forward against my every wish, dragging the rest of me with them.

I fall into the wheelbarrow. The tiny, fake wheelbarrow that certainly was not built to support an actual person.

The wooden planks give way almost immediately. My butt hits the floor with an all-too-loud thump. I suck in my breath.

With any luck—if I have any luck—I can manage to get up without getting stabbed by splinters.

That's when I hear the snickers.

It isn't the entire audience. At least I don't think so. But there are enough. And . . . and do I see people taking videos on their cell phones?

My face burns, and I know it has nothing to do with the heat of the spotlights still blazing down on me. I know with an awful feeling of certainty that everyone, absolutely everyone, is staring at me. They're thinking about how clumsy I am and isn't it so hilarious and of course the wheelbarrow broke under my weight, I'm *fat*.

I feel sick to my very core. A foul taste overwhelms my mouth. I . . . oh. Oh no.

I know what is going to happen, I can feel it starting. And yet I can't do a single thing to stop it.

I throw up over the wheelbarrow ruins. The distinct scent of raspberry lemonade–flavored vomit fills my nose, making me gag.

Ten seconds, or perhaps ten minutes later, I come to my senses. I leap to my feet. By some small miracle, I manage not to stumble or stab myself on splinters.

Then I run backstage.

Ms. W rushes over to me and starts to say something, but I don't hear a single word. Echoes of the jeering audience

ring through my skull, a looping soundtrack for my misery. I search the sea of people for the two faces I most want to see right now. My moms.

I don't find them, but I do manage to spot the next-best thing. Chloe. She's standing close to the stage, no doubt ready to make her next entrance. I try to meet her eyes, but she looks away. I can't quite figure out what her expression means—the quirk of her lips, the downcast eyes.

"Uh, hi," she says finally.

"Hi," I repeat. I'm not sure I'm capable of coming up with an original script right now.

A too-long pause lingers in the air. After what feels like eons, she speaks again. "Look. That was bad. But there's still time to save the show. You just have to do a really good job from here on out."

I frown as the implication of her words hits me. Save the show? That's what she cares about? The show?

I'm not sure I want to hear more from Chloe, not right now, but she keeps talking anyway. "Do you remember the hand trick I taught you?"

A fog descends on my brain, fast as one of Ms. W's dance numbers, and if I ever knew anything about Chloe's hand trick, I definitely don't right now. "I don't care about your stupid hand trick," I tell her. The edge to my voice surprises me. I don't talk like that to Chloe, or at least, I didn't used to.

"I'm just trying to help! Come on, Mads, you can totally do this. You can get this right."

"No. I can't," I say.

123

I want to say more—I need to say more, but words won't come out. Only awful, heaving sobs.

"Come on," Chloe repeats. She looks like she would prefer to be anywhere but here. Well, that makes two of us. "Don't ruin the show for everyone! Not again."

All of a sudden, I am painfully aware of the fact that my backside is still sore from my fall. That I'm still wearing the awful, too-small dress. That my eyes are becoming watery, threatening to destroy the layers of thick stage makeup.

"Well," I say. "I certainly don't mean to ruin the show. That would be just terrible, wouldn't it?"

I don't bother trying to hold in my sarcasm. Chloe deserves all of it and more.

Chloe winces, but only slightly. "Look, that came out wrong. Sorry. I just don't have the space to deal with this right now."

Fire erupts in my veins, and suddenly it is hard to see straight.

"Don't trouble yourself," I tell her. "You don't have to *deal with me* right now if you don't want to."

She opens her mouth to say something. Before she can, someone yells, "Your cue, Chloe!"

Right. Somehow, in the middle of everything, I almost forgot that the performance is still going on. Of course, Chloe hasn't forgotten any such thing. She pats down her hair and smooths out a nonexistent wrinkle on her dress. Then she marches back onstage as if absolutely nothing were wrong. I guess nothing is, for her.

I try my very best, but I cannot stop the flood of tears

that continues to gush down my cheeks. If my makeup wasn't completely ruined before, it is now. I should stop crying, I know I should. But I can't.

In my head, Chloe's voice taunts me. *You're ruining the show. I can't deal with this. I can't deal with you.*

"Shut up," I say to my best friend, who is no longer there.

Chloe

I messed up. I know I messed up. What I don't know is how to fix it.

I tried talking to Maddie after the show ended. Really, I did. But when I left the stage a whole crowd of people came over to congratulate me, and I couldn't exactly tell them to go away. So I talked to them, just a bit, and once I was done I looked for Maddie. But she was gone.

Over the weekend, I start to write like ten million texts to her. I delete every single one. They aren't good enough. I'm not being cowardly. It's just that I need to explain myself face-to-face.

Or at least, that's what I tell myself.

Maddie probably doesn't want to talk with me anyway. Not when the situation keeps getting worse and worse. A video of her fall started going around social media. Apparently it started like five seconds after she threw up, while we were still trying to power through the rest of the musical. When I last checked, the stupid video had 187,189 views. I flagged it for "inappropriate content."

I guess that's just about all I can do right now.

On Monday, I get to school earlier than usual. I want to be there for Maddie. Okay, yeah, I don't know what I'm going to say. Doesn't matter. I'll have to figure that out in the moment.

This whole dealing-with-other-people's-emotions issue is so not my thing. But I guess I have to try. For Maddie.

I wait by a scraggly eucalyptus tree, our unofficial before-school meeting spot. No Maddie, not even when most everyone else has started pouring into the school building. I wait some more.

Two minutes before first period starts, I have no choice but to admit that Maddie isn't coming. I race to class and try to ignore the lump in my throat.

I expect Maddie to be in social studies class. She isn't.

She isn't there on Tuesday, either. Or Wednesday.

By now, my nerves about the whole thing are worse than ever. At this point I'm pretty sure Maddie isn't actually sick. She just feels embarrassed about what happened and the video and everything else. And she's mad at me. Obviously. I get that. I really do. But still. She'll have to come back sooner or later. When she does, I am going to talk with her. I am going to say the things I should have said before.

On Thursday, I catch a glimpse of her on the way to first period. A few kids snicker at her when she walks by in the hallway. Some mean names get thrown around. Like "Maddie Barfins," which is the most uncreative thing ever. I give everyone who says that a long glare.

At least no one is playing that stupid video anymore. For the first few days this week every single jerk in this school was playing it constantly. Our school is at least 50 percent jerks, so that was really bad, obviously. But I talked to the principal about it, and now anyone who is caught playing the video gets detention. Most people don't take the risk.

Now that Maddie is back, I try to find a good time for us to talk. Problem: A good time never comes. She doesn't wait for me before class. She doesn't sit next to me at lunch. I don't see her in the cafeteria at all.

By Friday, I've reached the obvious conclusion. Maddie is avoiding me on purpose.

Fine. If she won't come to me, I'll go to her. I make a plan.

Maddie has art class last period on Fridays. I have gym, technically, but it's super easy to slip out early. As I walk to the art room, I take deep breaths. I still don't know exactly what I should say.

I wait by the doorway. One by one, kids sprint out of the room. I don't care about any of them, though. My attention is otherwise occupied. Finally, I see her.

Despite the fact that it's Friday, the best day of the entire school week, she looks not happy. Her hair is pulled back into a ponytail, like she couldn't be bothered to do anything else with it.

She sees me. I know the exact moment it happens because she starts to bolt.

I leap in front of her before she can get away.

"We need to talk," I say.

Her face scrunches up. I know she's remembering the last time we talked. Every stupid word that blurted out of my stupid mouth.

"I don't know if that's a good idea."

I ignore that. She has to listen to me. She just does. "I wanted . . . I wanted . . . I . . . I wanted to say that I'm . . . you know . . . sorry. I am so, so sorry."

Ack, why are my words coming out all garble-y? This is not how I wanted everything to go. I can only hope she can tell how much I mean it. How I really am sorry. Sorrier than I can even begin to express. But it isn't enough. I know it. I can see it in Maddie's crinkled forehead and snarly lip.

"Sorry for what?" she asks me.

"Uh . . ."

I stumble over my words. Again. I so wish there was a script for this, some magic lines I could say to make everything better. There isn't.

"You said you were sorry." Maddie's voice is quiet but firm. "What are you sorry for?"

Ugh, what kind of question is that, even? Doesn't Maddie already know the answer? But I guess I have to say it.

"For . . . for saying everything that I said. I didn't really mean it!"

I said it. Now maybe Maddie can forgive me. Can't she?

But she just crosses her arms over her chest. If anything, her scowl has intensified. "You said you would be there for me if anything bad happened."

"I . . . I tried! I tried to help!"

It's true. Okay, maybe my way of helping wasn't the best. I can see that now. But I did try. I can't help that I'm no good at the whole emotional comfort thing. Maddie's my best friend! She should know that about me. She should know I'm trying my best.

Still, I said the wrong thing. Again. Maddie clenches her jaw, and I almost shrink beneath her gaze. Before this very

moment, I didn't even know Maddie could glare like that. I definitely didn't expect her to glare like that at *me*.

Maddie doesn't speak for the longest time. When she does, her voice is vicious. "You said that I ruined the show. Is that your idea of help?"

"You're not being fair!" I tell her. Probably not the best thing to say, but it's how I feel. "I thought I could give you helpful advice. On, you know, dancing. And I had to go back onstage in five minutes so it's not like I had time for a whole big emotional talk or anything, you know . . ."

My voice trails off. I almost definitely made things worse. Still. I had to say what I feel!

"Right. You had to perform. Because it's always about you. Isn't that right, Chloe?"

"What's that supposed to mean?" Now *I* cross my arms.

Maddie shakes her head. "Chloe, maybe you haven't noticed, but our entire friendship is about you and what you want. When you want to show up, you show up. When you don't want to bother with me, you don't. When you want to go shopping, we go. Even if the stores you like don't even carry clothes my size! And when you want to be in the musical, I have to do it, too. Just so you can use me to get rides. You don't care that I have dyspraxia. You don't even acknowledge it. It doesn't matter, so long as you get whatever it is you want. I'm just another accessory to you. You don't care about me. You don't even care that everyone in the whole world saw that . . . that . . . *video*. You got to be the star and have people fawning over you, and that's what's important, right?"

130

Maddie says all that without pausing to take a single breath. I stare at her and try to take it all in. Maybe there's something to what she's said, okay, but a lot of her accusations feel unfair. It wasn't my fault that horrible video went viral! I tried to stop it. And how did I make Maddie do anything? She agreed to do everything I asked! It's not like I forced her to do the show. Also, I didn't even know some of this stuff, like how my stores don't have clothes that fit her. How am I supposed to know about any of this if she won't tell me?

"Of course I care about you! How can you even say that?" I ask.

"I don't know, Chloe. Maybe the same way you can say that I'm ruining the show for everyone."

At that moment I start to think that I really might lose her. I try to keep my voice calm, even though I feel anything but. "That was a mistake. I said I was sorry. But . . . Maddie . . . you agreed to be in the musical. I didn't make you do anything!"

"Yes, you did! You begged and manipulated me into it. But I'm done. I'm done being the supporting character in the movie of your life."

"I never asked you to—"

"You asked me a hundred times. And I always said yes. But not anymore."

"I . . . I said I was sorry," I repeat.

"Sometimes sorry isn't enough," Maddie says. Her voice is harsh. Very un-Maddie-like.

I blink. All of a sudden, the surrounding world feels blurry and uncertain. Nothing is how it should be.

131

"Do you mean . . . do you mean you don't want to be friends anymore?" I ask in my smallest voice.

Maddie blinks. She doesn't answer right away. But when she does, her voice leaves no room for doubt.

"Yes. That is exactly what I mean."

No. This absolutely cannot be happening. Maddie doesn't *really* mean she wants all of it to end—our sleepovers, our notes in class, our ongoing text thread. We've been best friends since forever. And yeah, I messed up, but she always forgives my mess-ups.

Except that now she won't. She looks like she's about to turn away. I can't let that happen.

"You won't have any other friends," I say before she can go. "Not without me."

I bite down on the inside of my lip so hard it aches. Out of all the things I could have said, why did I say that? It was the worst possible thing I could have done.

Fix it, Chloe. I have to fix it. I try to find the words, but Maddie beats me to it.

"I'd rather have no friends than a friend like you. Goodbye, Chloe," she says.

She leaves. I don't.

I wait by the doorway for her to come back, to say that maybe we can work this out. But she never does.

CHAPTER ELEVEN

Maddie

NOW: JULY

The surrounding forest is beautiful enough for a movie. Fluffy clouds in a perfectly blue sky break through a canopy of towering trees. I may not be thrilled about this afternoon's activity, kayaking in the lake. But with this kind of scenery, I can almost understand why some people love the outdoors.

At the moment, my biggest problem is my shoes. I'm wearing sandals. I didn't exactly want to wear sandals for traipsing through the woods, but I didn't have a choice in the matter. When I woke up this morning, my sneakers were full of thick, disgusting goop—shaving cream plus shampoo, I think. Chloe's doing, of course. She wanted revenge for the snake incident, and she got it.

I spent ages trying to clean out my shoes, and now they're soaking wet. They could be ruined forever for all I know, leaving me without my very favorite pair. I now need to retaliate in response to Chloe's retaliation. It's not just a matter of pride, truly. I need inspiration for my screenplay.

After my first prank on Chloe, I wrote a scene where Adina summons magical snakes to attack her traitor friend Eunice. But then I got stuck. Chloe's little prank helped me figure things out. Eunice, in response to the whole snake thing, attacks Adina with some kind of purple potion. Nothing can pierce Adina's clay skin, of course, but she is weakened. Now she needs to make her next move.

I try to think about the possibilities for payback while I walk, but I struggle to concentrate. For some reason, my eyes keep wandering to the other kids. Almost everyone in Cabin 7B has broken up into pairs and groups, including Chloe.

But not me. The window for making new friends at camp has seemingly closed shut.

You won't have any other friends, Chloe's voice whispers in my mind, with a viciousness that even the real Chloe never had. *Not without me.*

I'm so deep in feeling sorry for myself that I don't even mind when Mara taps me on the shoulder. While she may not be my favorite person, to put it mildly, at least she's talking to me.

You're pathetic, the voice pipes up again.

Mara snaps me out of my spiraling thoughts by pointing at my shoes. "Chloe messed up your shoes today, right?" she asked. "I saw you this morning."

I grind my teeth. "Yes. She did."

"Poor you," she says in a cooing voice.

The sympathy only annoys me even more. I mean, I'm not a helpless victim in all of this. I did prank Chloe first. Although, it should be noted, my prank did not involve ruining Chloe's property. I would never do something so mean.

I shrug at Mara. "She was just returning the favor. I pranked her with a prop snake the other day. She hates snakes, you know."

134

Mara lets out a *hmm* noise. "I didn't know that. Very interesting."

For some reason, her interest encourages me. I continue talking. "I'm doing a . . . a project, I guess you'd call it. I'm working on a screenplay."

"What kind of screenplay?" Mara asks.

I decide not to tell her the details of my plot and how I want to write about Jewish myths and everything. She wouldn't understand, I'm sure of it. Instead, I say, "I'm still working out the details. That's why I . . . anyway. Have you ever heard of method acting?"

"Yeah! That's when an actor pretends to be like their character in real life, right? Like if their character is Italian, they start speaking with an accent all the time."

"Right." I pause. "Well, I'm doing what you might call method screenwriting."

Mara's face twists in confusion at first, but after a moment, she gets it. She laughs. "Oooh. So, you're doing pranks on her to . . . to get inspiration for your screenplay?"

I grin. "Exactly."

"That's brilliant!"

We walk in silence for several moments before Mara speaks again. "I want in on your next prank, whatever it is. Maybe I can even help come up with some ideas, you know?"

My smile evaporates. "Why?" I ask her.

"Because I don't like Chloe. Like, really, really don't like her."

Chewing on the edge of my lips, I consider the new plot development. On the one hand, a little help would be very

useful. I need to do something more than plant a snake prop in Chloe's bed. On the other hand, do I really trust Mara? And do I even want to work with her?

Mara continues, now in a full-fledged tirade. "If you ask me, someone needs to teach that girl a lesson. She isn't so special just because she was on some stupid TV show."

By reflex, I open my mouth to say that Chloe doesn't think she's special just because she was on TV. But the defense dies in my throat. All the scenes from this spring replay themselves in my mind, over and over again.

Me, finding The Video while curled up in bed.

Me, walking down the hallway while some jerk yells "barf girl!"

Me, seeking comfort from Chloe while she coolly informs me that I ruined everything.

I open my mouth to say that Mara can forget about it, that I don't want anything to do with her.

Instead, I say, "Thanks. I'll think about it."

Thoughts of Chloe and Mara and what I ought to do next gnaw at me as we complete the journey to the lake. All of it makes my limbs jittery.

I am almost glad that we'll be kayaking. Sure, there are a dozen different ways such an activity could end in complete humiliation, but at least that will distract me from everything else.

As the counselor points us toward the life vests and starts explaining what we are going to do, a new worry crawls into my head. The kayaks are obviously for two people. I am

going to have to partner with someone or other. I bounce from one foot to another and fiddle with the straps on my life jacket. At least I found one in my size.

"So, I know you want to be with your friends," says Andy, the boating counselor, once we're all suited up. "But adventuring on a kayak is a great way to make new friends. Count off to seven, everyone!"

I know what that means. I could end up in a kayak with anyone—including Chloe. I try to remind myself that the odds of that happening are low. I don't know how low, exactly, since I hate math, but they are surely not high. Well, *probably* not high.

Everyone gathers into a loose line and starts counting off. I slip in toward the end of the line. Chloe, I notice, is number four. Once someone says number seven, the cycle starts again. I quickly count off in my head to prepare myself. One, two, three . . .

Oh.

I am number four.

When my turn comes, I try to stay calm. I manage not to look directly at Chloe. Maybe if I pretend she's just another girl from my cabin, I can get through this.

Before I can force my face into an expression that says "I don't care," Chloe marches up to me. I cross my arms and Chloe winces ever so slightly. She smiles—one of her fake smiles, of course. I am quite sure she isn't any happier about this arrangement than I am.

"Ready for your grand adventure?" Andy asks once we reach the front of the line.

"Totally," Chloe says.

I only manage a short nod.

On Andy's cue, Chloe slides into the back seat. I didn't really pay that much attention to Andy's whole explanation, but I'm pretty sure he said that the person in the back should call the shots. Obviously, that's Chloe. The kayak sways slightly under her weight, but she still manages to maintain her balance.

Now it's my turn. I take a deep breath and force my foot into the kayak. Almost immediately, I lose control of my legs. I can feel myself falling, slipping toward the murky lake and—oh gosh, I cannot fall in front of everyone. Not again.

Andy reaches out a hand, and I grab on to it. Somehow, I manage to make it into the seat with his help. It is not a particularly hopeful beginning to the adventure, but I am dry. And at least I don't have to look at Chloe anymore.

Andy grins his excited counselor grin. He unties the string attaching the boat to the dock and gives us a firm shove.

"Have fun!" he calls.

From behind me, Chloe snorts at such a ridiculous notion. I cannot help but agree with her.

CHAPTER TWELVE

Chloe

We drift away from the dock for several feet. Then, nothing.

I grip my oar. Even though I watched Andy's demonstration, now that I'm actually out here, the whole kayaking thing just seems way too complicated. Maybe we can go back. I can fake a convincing stomachache.

Of course, I'd still have to figure out how to move the stupid boat. I sigh and dismiss the idea. Maybe I don't like it, but we're out on the water now. I might as well try to steer us somewhere or other.

Annoyingly, Maddie isn't doing anything. Her oar sits on her lap untouched. Seriously, is she refusing to do this on principle or something?

"I guess we're supposed to row," I say.

Without saying anything, Maddie picks up her oar and starts rowing. We drift to the left.

"We both have to do it at the same time," I remind her. "One on each side."

She doesn't respond, but she stops moving the paddle. I guess I'll be taking the lead from here.

"I'll take the right side. You go left," I say. "Okay. One . . . two . . . THREE."

And with that, the boat shoots forward. It's not superfast or anything, but still. It feels like a victory.

"We did it!" I say. For a moment I forget that Maddie hates me.

"Yeah," she says. "We did."

"Look at us. Two city girls on a boat."

But as I talk, I guess I stop rowing the right way, because we start drifting aimlessly again. Oops.

"Chlo, I think you have to keep rowing," Maddie says.

She called me *Chlo*. A simple thing, maybe. Still, I can't help but think it means something. Maybe. I mean, before we got on the stupid boat she refused to talk with me at all. Using a nickname is definitely a step up. Maybe kayaking really is all of the things that Andy said it would be, weirdo that he is.

"Right," I say. "Sorry."

I begin rowing once again. For several minutes, we keep going at a steady pace. The wind at our back carries us forward, and soon we've reached the middle of the lake. My hair is falling out of my hair clip, but I can't fix it. My hands are glued to the oar.

Left.

Right.

Left again.

"Let's turn," I say.

After a bit of wrangling, we sync up our strokes and manage a smooth right turn. I still can't believe Maddie and I are doing this. Together.

Neither of us says anything more, but that's okay. I always liked this part of being with Maddie. The not having to say anything. I feel so happy about this turn of events that I want to sing.

So I do.

At first I am quiet, almost whispering to myself. But by the time I reach the first chorus of my chosen song, "Sit Down, You're Rockin' the Boat" from *Guys and Dolls*, my voice is loud enough for Maddie to hear.

"Are you singing?" she asks. I can't see her face, but I just know she's raising an eyebrow in that way she does.

"Yes. Want to join?"

"I don't know the words to that one. It's from an old-timey musical, right?"

"Yeah. *Guys and Dolls.* But we could sing 'Row, Row, Row Your Boat' instead."

Maddie laughs. The sound is so familiar yet so strange at the same time. I grin.

"Come on," I say. "I'll start."

"You will not."

"Row, row, row your boat gently down the stream . . ." I sing in my stage voice.

Maddie shakes her head, but a few lines in, she joins me. I think we sound pretty good together. We always do.

"This is kind of fun," Maddie says, sounding about as surprised as I feel. "Well, except for the part where my feet are gross and wet."

"Uh . . . sorry?" I say.

Maddie snorts. "You should be. It's your fault that I have to wear sandals."

I frown in confusion. Then, it clicks. "Oh, right. The shoes."

"Yes. The shoes."

141

A twinge of guilt pops up in my stomach. Ugh, how annoying.

"I didn't mean to, you know, *hurt* you or anything. I just wanted to get back at you for the snake."

It's the truth. I mean, yeah, I knew Maddie wouldn't be happy. And I knew those shoes were her favorite pair. But seriously, it was just a joke!

Anyway, she started it.

When Maddie speaks, her voice is hard. Unforgiving. "Well, now I can't wear those shoes for at least another day. If I'm lucky."

"I didn't think—" I begin to say.

"That's exactly the problem! Chloe, you never think. You just do what you want to do without thinking about anyone else, ever."

Anger starts to well up, pushing out the nagging guilt. How does Maddie get to act so high and mighty? Like she's perfect or something!

But I keep my cool. I don't say any of this.

"I'm . . . I'm sorry," I say.

Maddie grunts. Not a rejection, but not exactly a sign of *okay, let's be cool again*, either. I sigh inwardly. What do I have to do here?

I want to say something else. I should say something else. Maybe try to fix things. But I can't. Because we are now racing straight toward a rock. A big one.

"Left!" I yell. "Row left."

Maddie starts paddling again. That's the good part. The bad part is, she's paddling to the right.

"I said left! Seriously, this isn't hard."

She starts rowing on the other side. But by now it's too late.

Our kayak plows straight ahead. The kayak hits the rock with a loud *thunk*, and Maddie whimpers. I can feel the disaster unfolding, but I can't stop it. All I can do is watch.

Maddie's arms flail around. With the boat wobbling so much, she's lost her balance. And . . . and now she's tumbling sideways, straight into the lake.

I can't do anything.

As the boat sways, I barely manage to stay afloat myself. Thanks to the splash, the gross taste of lake water fills my mouth and nostrils.

"Are you okay?" I ask Maddie. Her round head bobs on the surface. She must be treading water to stay afloat.

I'm pretty sure she isn't in actual danger right now. We're both wearing life jackets, and anyway, Maddie can swim. Still, she glares at me as though I personally put the stupid rock in our path. She spits water out onto the nose of the boat.

"I just fell out of a kayak. No, I am not okay."

"Let me help," I say.

But Maddie shakes her head. "Don't bother."

I don't say another word. I extend a hand toward her. It will be tough, but maybe if we work together we can get her back up onto the boat.

She doesn't take my hand. Instead, she kicks her leg and starts to swim away from me. The dock isn't too far, so she should be able to make it.

I steer the kayak back to shore by myself.

CHAPTER THIRTEEN

Maddie

The moment I return to Cabin 7B, I race to the shower. I rub the shampoo into my scalp with so much vigor that it hurts. As though I can somehow wash away the humiliation along with the murky lake water and algae.

Once I'm in dry clothes, Chloe looks like she wants to approach me. But every time she comes close, I glare. That scares her off. She does not talk to me, and neither does anyone else. It is a bit lonely, if I'm being honest. Still, a little loneliness is better—much, much better—than another betrayal.

I flip open my notebook and try to work on my screenplay. I've already finished writing the magical snake attack and the fallout from that. Now I need something else. Closing my eyes, I try to summon the spirit of Adina. How does she feel after her once-friend betrayed her? Hurt, yes. Angry, obviously. The kind of anger that boils under your skin until it threatens to explode. Okay, but what is she going to *do*?

Just start writing, Maddie. Don't overthink.

At the top of the page I write, *EXTERIOR SCENE: A placid, glistening lake. Pan outward to towering trees.*

I frown. Where did that come from? I'm writing a story in London! Do they even have any lakes there? I don't know, but it doesn't matter. This isn't the story I want to write. It's just a product of my mind, replaying the disastrous events of this afternoon. Sighing, I put my notebook away. Maybe I'll write more later tonight.

But I don't. For the next day, I tiptoe through camp on high alert. Part of me expects a video of the kayaking incident to pop up on social media. True, the whole horrible thing happened in the middle of the lake, and the cell service here is unreliable to nonexistent. But as far as I'm concerned, you can never be too careful.

Luckily, there is no video, or even any mean nicknames. Most people just ignore me, like usual. For once I do not mind being alone.

Okay, so maybe the kids here are too nice or at least too busy to tease me about the kayak incident. But I remember what it felt like to fall into the lake. Just like I remember falling into the wheelbarrow. And every time I remember, I get mad at Chloe all over again. Maybe the accident wasn't entirely her fault, but I don't know if I particularly care. Besides, even if she hadn't caused the boat to crash, Chloe had done what she always does. She'd barked out instructions to me, mean and clueless as ever.

I said left! Seriously, this isn't hard.

Not hard for Chloe, maybe. I grind my teeth at the memory.

I try to forget all about it. I try to slip into Adina's mindset. When Adina gets hurt, she doesn't sit back and just let it happen. She *does* something about it, like the strong hero that she is.

Maybe I can do something, too.

Slowly, an idea comes to me. A completely terrible, awful,

just plain mean idea. Yet once it occurs to me, I cannot get rid of it.

If I am going to pull it off, I'll need some help. Unfortunately, there's only one candidate for the job. So what if it's my second-least-favorite person at camp?

I need time to think about it. Luckily, time is not in short supply. Tonight's activity is a real dud: a dance with a live band that plays really old music. I hang out on the fringes of the crowd. In the middle of the band's rendition of "Hound Dog," I make my decision.

I weave through a mass of sweaty, flailing bodies in search of Mara. I find her sitting in a corner alone. Her face lights up when she sees me.

"I have an idea," I say. "About how to get back at Chloe. But I'll need your help."

Mara raises a blond eyebrow and smiles at me. I do not think I like that smile, but I can't very well back out now. Or maybe I can—but I won't.

"Ooh. Do tell," she says.

I tell.

The rest of the dance passes in a blur. I don't dance, which leaves me plenty of time for thinking. If I were a movie character, I'd be having a Moment of Introspection. Admittedly, "Yellow Submarine" is not a musical number usually associated with Moments of Introspection, but I am having one anyway.

I search the crowd for Chloe. Even now I cannot help but look for her, I guess. I find her standing off in a corner,

146

arms crossed over her chest. I cannot see her face, but I can easily imagine the carefully blank expression. A Chloe specialty.

Sasha walks up to her. They talk, and a few minutes later Chloe joins the dance floor. So she already has a new friend. I am not surprised, exactly, but it still stings a bit. Am I that easy to replace?

I sigh. Really, I should be focusing on tomorrow, on what I have planned. A new scene that I can write however I please. Instead my mind keeps rewinding to other scenes, scenes from when Chloe and I were still friends. I can almost see our first day of kindergarten. It happened so long ago that I shouldn't remember it, but I do. Or at least I think I do. Either way, I can see the scene playing out, beat by beat.

Little Maddie wore pigtails and a dorky Merida T-shirt. Kids buzzed past me, talking and laughing, and of course I did not know any of them.

The teacher assigned seats. She led us in groups toward a cluster of desks, each with brightly colored squares pasted to the corners.

My desk had a blue square. Next to me, a girl with pretty red hair smiled. "I'm Chloe," she said. "I love your shirt. *Brave* is one of the best movies ever!"

And, just like that, all my jitters vanished. I smiled back at her. "Yes! It is."

"We are going to be best friends," Chloe said, as if there could be no possible question about the matter.

Even then, she didn't ask me if *I* wanted to be best friends

with *her*. But if she had, I would have said yes. I would have said yes a thousand times.

In the present scene, I fidget with my hands. Not for the first time, I wonder what would have happened if I had ended up at some other desk cluster. Or if I had worn a different T-shirt, even. More likely than not, Chloe and I would never have become friends. My entire life would have unfolded in a completely different way, all because of that one little thing.

It would have been better.

Still, another scene replays in my head. I'm at my eighth birthday—or was it my ninth? That's not really important, I guess. The important part was that nobody showed up. Nobody, that is, except for Chloe.

At first I thought people were just running late. I invented all kinds of excuses. The traffic was bad (very likely). Everyone had slept late by mistake (more of a stretch). A stampede of rhinos had escaped from the Los Angeles Zoo and were clogging up the freeways (okay, yes, that one was pretty far-fetched). But as the minutes slipped by, I had to face the facts. No one wanted to come to my birthday party, even though we had the most delicious ice cream cake.

Horrible, painful tears pressed against my eyes, threatening to spill out. I didn't want to cry at my own birthday party, but how could I not?

Mom and Sandra watched me, but didn't say much. I don't think they knew what to do, either. Chloe knew, though. Just like she always did.

"I didn't want to say anything," she said. "But I'm so glad none of those losers showed up."

I blinked, tears still threatening to burst from my eyes. "What? Why?"

She smiled at me—not the fake smile she gave TV cameras, but her real one. "Well, if other people were here, we couldn't play our secret game."

"What secret game?" I asked.

"The game you're going to come up with right now! You're the creative one. You'll make something great."

And that's exactly what I did. As it turned out, I didn't need other kids at my birthday party. Just Chloe.

The scene fades, and more images of Chloe and me drift across my mind's screen. *We are going to be best friends*, she had said.

I think of her cruel words backstage at the musical and her snappishness at the lake. I think of how she ruined my shoes.

"You broke everything first," I whisper to no one.

Then I shake myself and head toward the meeting place Mara suggested. Phase One of my plan is officially underway.

CHAPTER FOURTEEN

Chloe

"And now, I present . . . the announcements!"

Hannah gets really, really enthusiastic when she does the daily announcements. Like she's about to introduce Lin-Manuel Miranda's new musical or something. Camp Rosewood announcements are done with a video, which is kind of cool. Still, the whole thing is a little boring after a week and a half. I just want to get on with my real day.

I don't pay much attention as Hannah starts up the video. Instead, I rehearse "Popular" in my head. I really want to nail that song in rehearsals today. I know I can. Maybe if I add a little more emphasis to the second chorus . . .

Before I can finish my mental rehearsal, my face appears on the large screen. I can tell it's not recent footage, because my hair is longer than it is now. I gulp. How did I get up there? And is this what I think it is?

Oh. Oh no.

"Mom?" actor-me says on screen.

My hair is done up in a bun. It took forever for the stylist to get the right "messy but pretty" vibe down. I want to look away from myself, but I don't. I can't.

In the commercial, the actor who plays my mom smiles. "Honey, is something wrong?"

No. This absolutely cannot be happening. Why isn't

anyone putting a stop to this? I don't know how, exactly, this god-awful commercial ended up being played instead of the announcements, but it needs to stop. Now.

Actor-me hesitates before responding to my actor-mom. Just like the script said.

"I . . . I think I have my period."

At the mention of the word *period*, snickers break out. Not just among the boys, either. I want to scream that it's just a commercial, for love of everything not-holy. I was acting! Act. Ing.

Even though I want to run away, I force myself to keep my butt in the seat. I concentrate on keeping my face blank and boring. Someone did this to me. Whoever they are, I don't want to give them the satisfaction of seeing my embarrassment.

The stupid commercial continues for a bit. Actor-me whines about cramps. Right now, I think I'd prefer cramps to sitting here and watching myself. *Finally*, the screen flickers off. Blech, what took so long?

Hannah has returned to the front of the room. She looks super annoyed. That makes two of us. "As you can tell, we had a mix-up," she says. "I am incredibly disappointed in the person who is responsible for this. Whoever you are, you will be held accountable. Meanwhile, how about I read today's announcements? You guys are going to love tonight's evening activity . . ."

My cue to tune out.

I scan the room. I want to know who did this. No, I *need* to know who did this.

151

Soon enough, my eyes find Maddie. Her cheeks are really pink, and she fidgets with her hands. The same thing she always does when she's anxious. Well. That's my answer right there.

It shouldn't surprise me, really. But I still feel like someone kicked me into a mud pit while I was wearing my favorite pair of jeans. Maddie *knows* me. Better than anyone else, probably. She knows how much I hate that stupid commercial. So how could she do that to me? Do all our years of BFF-ship mean nothing to her?

I guess they don't. At least not anymore.

The announcements end, and so does breakfast. I don't care about any of it.

After I managed to keep it together during the commercial, I had every intention of ignoring Maddie for the rest of the day. And the rest of forever. Really, I did.

It's just . . . she's so close right now. After breakfast we're all stuck in the cabin together for cabin cleaning. I try to concentrate on cleaning duties, but she's taunting me with her presence. I swear, she just keeps looking at me while I make my bed.

So I march up to her. I keep my Calm Face on, or at least I think I do.

"How could you do this to me? You . . . you know how much I hate that commercial. And you did it anyway."

I didn't mean to say all that, but it just came out. Against my deepest wish, my voice cracks.

"I don't know what you're talking about, Chloe," Maddie says. She stares at the floor. Like that's so interesting.

"You're a terrible liar," I say. "If you're going to do something like that, you should at least be able to own up to it."

My Calm Face slips as I narrow my eyes and purse my lips. I can't help it. Of course, Maddie isn't even looking at me right now.

Finally, she pulls her head up. She doesn't meet my eyes. "You know why I did it."

I do. But it just doesn't feel fair.

"So it was payback for the musical. And the stupid shoes. And what happened with the kayak, which, by the way, was not my fault. But whatever. Fine. It's . . . don't you think that was a little much? Was what I did really bad enough to deserve something like that?"

I really, really try to keep my anger under control, like Chloe Winters is supposed to do. Despite my best efforts, I am almost shouting. I can just tell that the other kids in the cabin are looking at us now. Great.

Still. I don't regret saying what I did. Maybe a few people at camp had already seen the commercial, like Annoying Mara. Now? They all have. And maybe most of them are too nice to make fun of me for it to my face or anything like that, but now they know. They know that I'm not really cool and in control. I'm a girl who acted in a commercial about cramp pills.

There's no coming back from that.

"Under the circumstances, what I did was perfectly fair," Maddie says, although she doesn't sound too sure of herself. I notice that much. "You played a prank on me. My

153

shoes are still messed up, by the way, thanks for asking. So I returned the favor, and now we're even. Okay?"

No, not okay. Not even close to okay. But I absolutely cannot continue this conversation for even one more second. So I start to turn away—but not before saying one last thing.

"Well, Maddie, you got what you wanted. We are never, ever going to be friends again."

I walk away as fast as I can. I refuse to let her see the stupid, annoying tears prickling against my eyes.

For the first time since I came here, I want to go home. But I can't think about that right now. I won't. So I go back to cabin cleaning duties. Even though my bed is already neat, I straighten the corners of the sheets. At least those will be in exactly the right place.

As I finish up and start walking to rehearsal, I'm still in a fog. I can see everything around me, but I can't feel it. Not the way I normally do. I just keep replaying the video. How could Maddie do this to me?

I shake myself. Rehearsal is not the time for wallowing. I am an actor. Under my breath, I start singing "Let It Go" from *Frozen*. A babyish choice, yeah, but it fits.

Conceal, don't feel, I whisper-sing.

That's what I need to do.

By the time I reach the barn, I have slipped into full-on actor mode. Some kids stare at me and whisper. But I ignore them, thank you very much. They're just supporting actors.

Like usual, I find a quiet corner for my vocal exercises. At first my voice feels wrong and comes out all croaky. But with

every note I grow stronger, until I almost feel like myself again.

Sasha comes over and watches me with interest.

"You'll need to teach me how to do that sometime," she says.

"Sure," I say.

Right now, I'd agree to anything Sasha might ask. She isn't talking about the stupid commercial.

Audrey doesn't mention it, either. She's her usual self—all directions and criticism balanced with praise. I do my best to earn that praise. I shove everything aside. I try to become Galinda. Even though the part wasn't my first choice, I've appreciated it more since we started rehearsing. Galinda is sort of like me, in a way. No one ever really sees her. They just focus on the pink and the sparkly-ness.

Today so isn't my best rehearsal. I'm too distracted. Still, I'm almost disappointed when Audrey calls for a short break. I don't want to return to being Chloe, even if it's just for fifteen minutes.

Obviously I don't bother with the other cast members. I pull up a seat next to Sasha. She takes out a ball of yarn and two big knitting needles. It is such an old-lady hobby, but it suits her. I watch her needles clatter away.

"Do you want to learn?" she asks.

I blush. I don't know why, exactly. Sasha just makes me blush a lot. It's very annoying.

"Sure," I say. Actually, I don't care about knitting, like, at all. But I do want to spend more time with Sasha.

She probably wouldn't betray me. Not like Maddie. *Ugh, don't think about Maddie.*

Sasha says something else, but I don't catch it. She looks at me, expecting.

"I'm sorry," I say. "What?"

She shrugs. "Nothing important. I've been meaning to ask. Are you okay?"

"Of course I am. Why wouldn't I be okay?" I say at once. Then I wince. Sasha hasn't been anything but nice to me. I shouldn't snap at her like that. "I mean . . . sorry. You're right. I guess today hasn't been the best."

Sasha offers a tight smile. "That was awful, what happened to you," she says. "But you shouldn't be embarrassed. Actually, it's really cool that you were in a commercial."

I blush, again. Obviously I know that Sasha watched the commercial. But hearing her reference it . . . well, it makes me uncomfortable.

"That commercial is the opposite of cool," I say.

"Well . . . maybe it is a little embarrassing. But you're lucky to get any parts at all. I've been on a bunch of auditions and I haven't gotten anything. Ever."

"That's horse doo-doo. You're really talented."

I mean it. Most of the other kids here have no talent at all, but Sasha is different. I could totally see her in a movie, and not just one of those obscure indie titles no one ever sees. A big movie. She'd light up the screen.

She blushes. "Thanks. I guess maybe I just have to keep at it. But . . ."

"Yeah?"

156

Biting her lip, Sasha gestures at herself. "I'm not you. I'm a chubby, Mexican Jewish girl. It's sucky, but in Hollywood, that matters. You know how Hollywood is all about looks."

I know. And I remember Audrey saying something like that, too. I bite my lip and debate what to say next. I decide on the truth.

"Well, whatever Hollywood does, I think you're great. And . . . and really pretty, too."

Ugh ugh ugh. What possessed me to say *that*? I'm sure my face must match my hair by now. But if Sasha notices, she doesn't comment on it. She just smiles at me.

"Well, Chloe, I think you're great, too. And pretty."

Oh. Wow.

Calm down, Chloe. There isn't anything special about what Sasha said. Girls call other girls pretty all the time. It doesn't mean anything. And I'm . . . I'm not . . .

"Thanks," I say. My voice is barely more than a whisper.

That's when Audrey calls us back to rehearsal. Thankfully.

When the music starts up again, I try to become Galinda once more. But for the rest of the day, I can't quite look Elphaba—Sasha—in the eye.

Well. At least I have something to think about besides my ex–best friend.

CHAPTER FIFTEEN

Maddie

After the announcements, after what I did, I try to pretend that everything is normal, completely normal, why would it not be normal? But one thought keeps running through my mind. Chloe knows what I did. An uncomfortable lump lodges itself in my chest, aching and throbbing. No matter how much I try to wish it away.

Mara's presence only makes everything worse. I try to avoid her, but she's everywhere. During the prank, she gave me a more-than-slightly-evil grin, like we're partner villains in a movie. I suppose we are.

I'm not like you, I want to tell her. I am not! But I sort of am.

Chloe looks at me throughout the day, too. Only her faces include glaring eyes and pursed lips. I know I deserve it, but I don't enjoy it.

Her words keep echoing in my mind. *Well, Maddie, you got what you wanted. We are never, ever going to be friends again.* Is that really what I wanted, deep down in the crevices of my heart?

I honestly don't know.

Maybe we're never going to be friends again, but I want to apologize to her, I really do.

As I pick through the contents of my dinner—a meat-loaf of questionable origin—I try to summon my nerve.

Yesterday, I did something beyond nervy when I snuck into Hannah's office to mess with the announcements video. Yet this feels infinitely harder.

But I have to do it. I clear my tray and walk toward Chloe. She always sits at the same table, toward the back of the mess hall. Usually she's with her new best friend, Sasha.

As I walk over, words tumble around my brain. *I'm sorry. I didn't mean it.* But I did mean it, didn't I? And even a million sorries can't change that basic truth.

Before I can plop down next to Chloe, I am intercepted. Sasha. Her face twists into a scowl.

"We need to talk," she says.

Uh-oh. Sasha and I have never talked before, not really. Somehow I do not think this is going to go well for me.

"Yes?" I say.

"Leave Chloe alone."

I try to keep my breaths nice and even, despite the hot prickles coursing through my skin.

"That's my plan," I tell her, and I do mean it.

"Is it?"

Sasha glares at me so long and so hard that I very nearly shrink under her gaze.

Even though I can't defend what I did, I feel the need to defend myself anyway. Probably not very sensible of me, but since when have I been sensible when Chloe is involved?

"You don't know the whole story!" I say, my face hot. "She . . . she did stuff to me. Before camp. And she ruined my shoes!"

Yes, I am fully aware that what I did wasn't exactly a proportionate response to the shoe incident. No, I don't expect Sasha to have even a bit of sympathy for my plight. I guess I just had to say it anyway. Maybe I needed to prove that Chloe isn't some poor, helpless victim in all of this. I don't know.

Sasha gives me another withering glare. "Sorry. Well, no, I'm not. I don't actually care about your sad story. And I definitely don't care about your shoes. I just want to know that you're not going to hurt my friend from now on."

"I . . . I won't." My voice squeaks.

"Sasha."

A new voice—Chloe's. She must have marched over here while Sasha was scolding me.

Sasha's head snaps over to Chloe.

"Let it go," Chloe says. "It's . . . it's not worth it."

After a moment, Sasha nods. But she gives me another glare.

With that, Sasha flips her hair and turns away from me. My own feet remain firmly stuck to the ground. I stare at Chloe as she retreats back to her table. Her tray is full of food, but she hasn't touched any of it.

All of a sudden I remember why I'm here. I came over to apologize. So I should say something, anything. But the very thought feels absurd.

I flee.

For the first time in my memory, Chloe is uncomfortable onstage. I'm not sure anyone else even notices, but I do.

160

There's just something about the way she stands around with a pinched face, very much not in character. Galinda, after all, is always peppy. The song she's singing right now, "Popular," is the peppiest number of them all. Normally Chloe would be absolutely nailing it, but today everything is different.

"Let's try that one again," Audrey says.

I swear that Chloe almost grimaces, but she bobs her head into a nod.

"Elphie, now that we're friends, I've decided to make you my new project," she recites.

Sasha responds. "You really don't have to do that."

Next, Galinda is supposed to say, *I know. That's what makes me so nice.*

"I know," Chloe says. "That's what makes me so bad . . . I mean, good. I mean, nice."

Chloe's face flushes pink. She pauses, as if not knowing what to do next. I frown at such an unsettling scene.

"Continue," Audrey says.

After a not-quite-there moment of hesitation, Chloe breaks into song.

"Whenever I see someone more fortunate than I, and let's face it, who isn't, more fortunate than I . . ."

Less fortunate, I correct silently. Galinda thinks that everyone else is *less* fortunate than she is. The character is very much like Chloe, now that I think about it.

Audrey motions for Chloe to continue, but she doesn't. She pauses and lets out a word that most certainly is not in the script.

161

"Language!" Audrey says, though she isn't harsh.

"Sorry," Chloe mutters.

"Maybe we should take a break," Audrey says.

"No! I can get this right."

Audrey nods, though I don't think she looks particularly happy about it. Next to me, a girl I don't know well lets out a soft chuckle.

I give her a good, long glare. Really! What right does she have to laugh at Chloe? But as I look around, I realize that she's not the only one. Murmurs and giggles echo all around me. More than once, I hear the words "Cramp Girl."

"Guess she isn't so great at acting when she's not whining about getting her period," a familiar voice says loudly. Mara.

I squirm in my seat and clench my fists. This is my fault, I know it is. What I don't know is how to fix it.

And still a nasty little voice in my head whispers that at least Chloe's humiliation wasn't captured on video for 187,189 people to view.

Even so. I worked with Mara to embarrass Chloe, and with every minute that passes I regret that choice more and more. Onstage, Chloe plods through her dance. I can tell she just wants to get through it. Her kicks and twirls have none of her usual Chloe-ness. Sasha watches her closely. She's a good best friend for Chloe, I guess, certainly better than me.

The music cranks up to the big finish. "La la la!" Chloe sings.

She flails an arm in a dramatic gesture. Then she must

162

lean too far to the side because she trips and falls flat on her butt.

The entire crowd erupts into snorts. Chloe looks as though she wants to crawl beneath the floorboards of the stage and stay there for the next month.

I know the feeling.

Audrey whips her head around to face the crowd of snickering kids. "Enough! You will respect your fellow actors, or you just might find yourself washing dishes tonight."

That shuts everyone up, but Chloe still hasn't gotten up off the stage. She stares at the wooden stage, not daring to look up.

I have to admit, the viciousness with which everyone turned on her is surprising. I know why I'm mad at Chloe, but what problem do these kids have with her, really? Are they just jealous of her talent, her success?

Just like I am. It is an ugly, uncomfortable thought.

I should do something, anything. But at this point I have no idea what that something ought to be.

Audrey calls for another break. This time Chloe doesn't even try to argue.

I swallow. I am almost certainly making a mistake, but I have to do it. After checking that Sasha is nowhere in sight, I make my move. I approach Chloe.

"I'm sorry," I say the moment I see her.

She scowls. "You don't have to apologize just because you feel sorry for me at the moment, Maddie."

"I don't feel sorry for you," I tell her. Although I kind

163

of do. "I just . . . I messed up. With the whole commercial thing. I realize that now. I don't expect you to forgive me, but I had to say sorry."

"Is that why you did it?" she asks, folding her arms over her chest.

I don't know what I expected from her. I did not think she would actually accept the apology. But I definitely didn't expect this, whatever this is. I shift uncomfortably from one foot to another. It's too late to escape this conversation, but I still wish I could make a run for it.

"What do you mean?" I say finally.

"Did you want me to be humiliated? Is that why you did it?" she asks me.

I can't even bring myself to look at her. Because the answer is yes, of course. I did want her to be humiliated. She knows it, I know it, everyone at Camp Rosewood knows it.

"I . . . I'm sorry," I say again.

This time, she's the one who walks away from me.

I force myself to stop looking at her. Desperate for a distraction, I grab my screenwriting notebook. After all, I am supposed to be working on my screenplay. That was why I did the whole ridiculous prank in the first place, wasn't it? I am going to write a fantastic screenplay, something that will make Hannah sit up and take notice and tell me that I'm destined for a career in Hollywood.

If I can only figure out what happens next.

I try to put myself in Adina's shoes. She wanted revenge against her traitor friend, didn't she? Just like I did. And I got it. What now?

Closing my eyes, I try to transport myself into the as-yet unwritten scenes. I try to come up with something, anything, to scribble down in the notebook. But all I can see is Chloe's grimace.

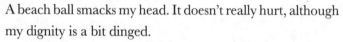

CHAPTER SIXTEEN

Chloe

A beach ball smacks my head. It doesn't really hurt, although my dignity is a bit dinged.

"Can you just *not*?" I ask the group of kids responsible for the damage.

Right now we're in free time. So we can do whatever we want. But still. I'd like to avoid flying projectiles, thanks.

"Sure thing," one of them says.

". . . Cramp Girl," another kid adds. Not quietly, either.

The rest of the group snickers and my cheeks burn. Even though it's been four days since Maddie's little prank, people are still using that stupid nickname. So ridiculous. And also humiliating.

I glance toward Sasha. She sits next to me, working away at her knitting. I really hope she didn't hear the Cramp Girl thing, but the curl of her lip indicates that she did.

"What a bunch of jerkwads. My eight-year-old cousins are more mature than that," she says once the jerkwads in question are gone.

"Yeah," I say. But my face is still on fire.

Sasha gives me a slight smile. "You really shouldn't be so embarrassed about the commercial, you know."

I stare into the blades of grass and wish for a way out of this conversation.

"I'm not embarrassed," I say. A lie. "I just don't want to keep taking about it. It's not that interesting! Like, can we just move on?"

Sasha nods. "Yeah, I get that. But the way some people are acting is ridiculous. I mean, hello, some people have periods and cramps. It's a natural process! Why make such a big deal about it?"

I shrug. "It is an embarrassing commercial."

"Only because our society is so weird about this stuff! Did you know that in Mexico some people do a special ceremony when you get your period for the first time? It's like a special ritual that welcomes you into being a woman. I read a book about it."

Maybe Sasha is right. Maybe I'm just embarrassed because of society and stuff. Still, all this period talk is making me itchy. So I open my mouth to suggest that we go grab frozen yogurt at the canteen, maybe, but Sasha speaks first.

"We don't have to do period talk. But can I ask you something, Chloe?"

I gulp. No one ever asks that question when they're going to say, "What do you think about the movie adaptation of *Rent*?" or whatever. I nod anyway.

"Why does your friend from school hate you so much? I mean, your former friend."

"Maddie?" I ask. But of course she means Maddie, because duh.

"Yeah. Her."

"It's . . . it's complicated," I say. 100 percent true.

"Try me."

167

I take a deep breath. If I tell Sasha everything that happened between Maddie and me, she might hate me. I do it anyway. When I finish, I start examining my hands.

"And that's why Maddie wanted to humiliate me, I guess," I say.

"You still don't deserve to be called Cramp Girl."

"But I am a terrible friend. Aren't I?"

She shrugs. "That's not for me to decide. At least not with Maddie. You've been a good friend to me."

Again, I blush. Again, I try to ignore it. "Thanks."

Sasha looks like she wants to say more, but I've totally had enough emotion talk for one afternoon. For several days, in fact. I leap up.

"Come on," I say. "It's Froyo day."

Fifteen minutes later, we're sitting at a table in the canteen. I take a spoonful of my yogurt—strawberry and chocolate chips. I watch Sasha dive into her own cup.

I've done stuff like this a million times with Maddie. With Sasha . . . it's different. I don't know why, but it is.

"It's so cool that you were in *The Music Man*," Sasha says.

Even though I don't really like that subject these days, I nod. "Yes. I was Marian the librarian. Maddie says stuff that happens to her is sexist, but it's the lead role."

"Why do I get the idea you'd happily play a serial killer if she were the lead?"

I grin a bit sheepishly. "I do like to be the star. So, yeah, I'd take a serial killer part if she has a decent ballad."

"No judgment from me. I'm a certified diva myself," she says. "But also . . ."

She shifts in her seat.

"Yeah?" I ask.

"I know this is kind of a weird question, but did you kiss a boy? In the musical?"

I think back to my awkward kisses with Carlos and nod.

"What was it like?" Sasha asks. "Kissing a boy?"

I shrug. "His lips were chapped."

Really, I just don't have much to say on the subject.

Sasha laughs. "Sorry. I know it's kind of a weird question. It's just that all of my friends back home have kissed people, and I haven't. And I'm totally cool with that, but I'm wondering what it's like."

"To me, it wasn't a real kiss," I tell her. "It was just part of the show. Acting. You're going to do a stage kiss with the boy who plays Fiyero, right?"

Sasha looks away once more. "Yeah. I guess I will."

I try not to show my own nerves about the sudden change in topic. Sasha and I are actors, and kissing is part of the job. There's no reason to be so weird about it, really.

She lifts a spoon of Froyo to her mouth, and I watch. Maybe all the kissing talk has infected my brain or something, but as she licks her lips I wonder all of a sudden what it might be like to kiss Sasha. Nothing like kissing Carlos, I'm sure.

Right now her lips look so soft and pink and . . . and . . .

I think I might like kissing Sasha.

Oh.

I like Sasha. Just like I liked Kaitlyn from social studies class this year. I like girls.

Cordelia's voice whispers in my ear, nagging me even though she's hundreds of miles away. *People might think you're a lesbian or something.*

I look at Sasha, so pretty with her dark hair and long eyelashes and okay, yeah, of course I've noticed that she has boobs. She's . . . she's Sasha. Pretty, wonderful Sasha.

In my head, I respond to my mother. *What if I were a lesbian? Would that be so bad?*

"Uh, Chloe?" Sasha says. A little bit of vanilla frozen yogurt has ended up on her chin. I resist the urge to reach over and wipe it off for her.

"Yes?" I respond after a long pause.

"You kind of spaced out there for a minute," she says.

"Oh. Uh, sorry."

"It's fine. Anything interesting happen? In your head, that is."

"I'm just going over the end of act 1," I tell her.

A total lie. But I'm not about to share my actual thoughts with Sasha, of all people.

She accepts my explanation, and we start talking about musical stuff. Even then, I keep circling back to my other thoughts. Now that I've considered what it might be like to kiss Sasha, I can barely manage to think of anything else.

I wish so much I could talk to someone about this . . . this whatever. This terrifying but strangely wonderful explosion of feelings.

I try to act it all out in my brain. *Maddie, I like girls,* I say. *And I especially like Sasha.*

There's no use denying it: Maddie is the person I want

right now. She wouldn't judge me, or try to talk me out of it. She would just listen and smile. Maybe ask me if I wanted to hug it out. (I'm not usually much of a hugger, but I'd say yes.)

Of course, none of that is going to happen. Ever. Maddie has made it super clear that she doesn't want to talk with me again. And really, after what she did, I shouldn't want to talk with her, either.

But I do.

CHAPTER
SEVENTEEN

Maddie

Five days have passed since I betrayed Chloe—five very long and mostly unpleasant days. Chloe hasn't said a word to me since the day it happened, and I am beginning to think she never will.

Truly, I deserve it.

The only person who is at all inclined to talk with me anymore is Mara. Now that we committed a crime together, she thinks we're friends, I guess. I don't know how to convince her otherwise, so I've taken to avoiding her altogether. At least I have my screenplay to distract me. I've been working on it during every spare moment I can find. Although there are still some holes in the plot, I've added quite a few scenes. I think it's really starting to come together.

I can only hope Hannah agrees.

This morning's screenwriting class is extra special, and extra terrifying. Hannah is going to give me feedback on my screenplay, or at least ten pages of it.

Please let her like it. *Please please please.*

I bounce my leg a little as I wait for Hannah to begin our feedback session.

"Your character and concept are so refreshing," Hannah begins.

I smile. Maybe she's obligated to begin with a compliment.

In fact, I'm almost certain that she is. But I still savor the feeling.

She continues. "But if I'm being completely honest, I'm really not sure about why she started conjuring snakes. It felt a little like it came out of nowhere."

I blink. I thought that was obvious. "Because she wants revenge," I say slowly. "And because Chl—I mean, Adina's former friend—hates snakes."

Yikes, why did I almost say Chloe's name? I have got to hope Hannah didn't notice my mistake.

Hannah waves a hand. "Yes, I know that revenge is a big part of the plot. But you might want to rethink that."

"What? Why? Lots of superheroes are motivated by revenge!"

I don't want to be a jerk about this. I knew that Hannah would have criticism for me. But to question my—I mean, Adina's—entire motive? I definitely wasn't expecting that.

Deep breaths. Maybe I can still convince her that it's good. That *I'm* good.

"When we first talked, you said that Adina wanted respect," Hannah points out "That's different from revenge, isn't it?"

Frowning, I stare down at my hands. "I guess."

Hannah nods, apparently encouraged.

"Your ideas are so fresh, with the use of Jewish mythology and everything. Adina has the potential to be such a unique, well-realized character. She's smart, she's creative, she has this whole interesting thing of feeling like an outsider because of who she is. Why should she be just like every

other superhero in terms of her motivation? It just doesn't feel very narratively satisfying. Can't she have another goal? Something that she really, really wants?"

Something other than revenge? What else would Adina possibly want after she's been so wronged? Except . . . except . . .

I wanted revenge, too. I got it. I thought it was what I wanted. I thought it would take away all the awfulness and humiliation, make it hurt less.

Yet I was wrong, more wrong than I possibly could have imagined. Doing it just made me feel horrible, and pretty much ensured that Chloe will never want to be friends with me again.

As much as I hate to admit it, the whole thing just isn't *narratively satisfying*.

"I have to tell you something," I say.

Hannah raises her eyebrows in surprise, but motions for me to continue.

I take in a deep breath. If I am going to do this, I need to do it quickly.

"I'm the one who messed with the announcements last week," I say in a rush. "I wanted to get revenge on Chloe for . . . well, that isn't important."

Hannah looks at me for a moment, her lips pursed. Then she nods.

"Thank you for your honesty," Hannah says.

I fidget with my pen. "I guess I thought that revenge would feel good, but it really didn't."

"Maybe that can be in your screenplay."

174

Weirdly, the thought makes me excited. "I hadn't thought about that."

Hannah nods at me. "Please do. In fact, you can think about it while you wash dishes at the mess hall for the next two weeks."

I don't try to argue. I know very well I deserve that and more. Honestly, I'm glad I came clean to Hannah. The knot in my stomach feels just a little bit looser, for the first time since last week.

Staring at the pages of my screenplay, I turn to Hannah.

"I think maybe Adina doesn't want revenge after all. You're right. It's a cliché."

The moment I speak the words, I feel their truth.

"Well. Then what's her big goal?" Hannah asks.

"I don't know."

For the next day, I think about my screenplay and make absolutely no progress. I can't even decide where my next scene ought to take place. Then, Audrey makes an announcement that makes my skin prickle.

"Good news, troubadours. The costumes have arrived!" she says.

My breaths start coming out funny, and I dig my fingernails into my palms. Somehow, I had forgotten all about costumes until this very moment. I guess I assumed we'd be wearing our own clothes. Obviously a mistaken assumption on my part. I force myself to breathe more slowly and focus on Audrey.

"Every day, you've all gotten a little closer to inhabiting

your roles. But to really and truly become the witches and wizards and nonbinary magicians of Oz, you will need to be decked out in . . . wait for it . . . magical robes!"

Audrey says this like it's some kind of wonderful revelation, but I frown. Camp started less than two weeks ago. When did they have time to order a bunch of robes? I don't remember telling anyone my size! And I would remember that, I know.

"We bought costumes in a range of different sizes, so you can pick out your own!" Audrey tells us. "Find a robe that speaks to you, something that makes you feel powerful and magical and ready to nail your performance."

She goes on for a bit about the importance of costumes and identity and becoming the character. I do not care. I can barely even see straight as she leads us over to the clothing racks that have been set up backstage.

Everyone else oohs over the brightly colored robes, but not me. I bite my lip and consider. *Will any of these things fit me?*

The moment Audrey gives the go-ahead, kids start grabbing robes. I can tell by sight that most won't fit me. Almost everyone here is smaller than I am. Still, I search the racks and look for something that might be me-sized.

I consider a purple robe that's a bit bigger than the others—no, no, not right. Then I look at a pretty emerald green costume, but discard it when I realize that it looks larger on the rack than when I hold it up to my body.

Darting my eyes around, I hope and hope that no one is watching me. For once, they're not. The other kids are too

busy for that. They spin around in their new robes, squealing and admiring themselves. My jaw hardens. I know it isn't intentional, but their happiness kind of feels like showing off to me.

Finally, I see a robe that might fit me. It happens to be ugly and orange. Well, I guess I can't be picky.

I put one arm through the armhole, then the other. When I try to close the robe across my chest, I only manage one of the hooks. I don't dare attempt any of the other fasteners. I could break it, and how would that look to everyone?

The robe's fabric pulls across my stomach, but it doesn't rip. I guess if I had to wear this for the performance, I could do it, even if I don't know how I'll move the upper half of my body.

I try so hard not to cry. I remind myself what Mom and Sandra tell me every time we visit a store that doesn't carry anything in my size. "You are beautiful, baby," Mom always says. "This store obviously doesn't deserve our business if they can't be bothered to make something for you."

Still, that never quite works, not completely, and here there are no moms to soothe me. There isn't an option to just order something online, either. It's the tight orange robe or nothing.

I lift an arm to get myself out of the awful costume. Even that slight movement causes the fabric to strain and . . . oh. Oh no.

With a faint *screech*, the fabric begins to tear.

I am extra careful as I continue taking off the robe. I barely allow myself to breathe. Finally, I escape the robe.

The tear is still there, though—an ugly reminder that I am too fat for this costume. Not the right fit for this musical and this world.

I shove the robe back onto its hanger and try to convince myself that no one saw. No one will know what happened. Still, tears stab my eyes and I absolutely cannot stand to be here for another second. So I run toward the bathroom.

The door is propped open by the chair. I want the satisfaction of slamming a door, so I remove it. Giving the door a good slam helps, if only a little.

I make for the nearest stall so I can wallow in peace, but something stops me. The sound of sniffles. Someone is already crying in the bathroom. I frown. Well, this is awkward. But I suppose I can stay here, just for a bit.

Then I spot the black and pink sneakers underneath the door to the stall, and I know. I know those shoes.

"Chloe? Is that . . . is that you?"

CHAPTER EIGHTEEN

Chloe

I am in the bathroom crying.

Because I have a problem. Namely, my underwear is red. Red brown. Whatever you want to call it.

With my eyes closed, I try to take slow, deep breaths. I only sort of succeed.

I know what this means. Obviously. I have my period, for the first time ever. What I don't know is how I'm supposed to deal with the whole sucky situation. It's not like I have pads and tampons conveniently tucked away in my bag.

And even if I do figure out the whole bleeding-in-my-underwear problem . . . then I'll just have to go back to rehearsals. Back to Sasha.

Everything had been going so well today. Audrey told us about the costumes, and I went backstage with Sasha and cooed over all the pretty robes. I picked out a pink robe, of course. Pink is Galinda's color. But then *it happened*.

After twirling around for a bit, I placed the robe back on its hanger. That's when Sasha's smile became a grimace.

"Um, Chloe?" she said.

"What?" I asked. My first thought was that maybe I had broccoli stuck in my teeth or something. If only.

"You, uh . . . I think you have your period."

Sasha pointed to my shorts. My *white* shorts. A large red

stain had bloomed in my, *ahem*, private area. Since I am the most unlucky person on the planet, I was wearing shorts made out of silky material. *White* shorts. Meaning the red spot grew super quick, forming a bull's-eye on my you-know-what.

Because I guess it isn't bad enough that half of Camp Rosewood thinks of me as Cramp Girl. Now I have to advertise *I just got my period and I'm not prepared for it* on my shorts.

I didn't say anything. I couldn't possibly. I just raced toward the bathroom stall. That was maybe fifteen minutes ago.

So now I've got three major problems. Number one, I have my period. Number two, my shorts are ruined, prob-ably forever. And, worst of all, number three. I humiliated myself in front of Sasha. The girl I *like*.

It's way too much and I don't know what to do and before I even realize what I'm doing I start to cry. Not the delicate, pretty tears directors like. More like great heaving sobs and snot getting all over the place and all that grossness.

Then I hear a voice.

"Chloe? Is that . . . is that you?"

I know that voice. Right now, I'm not sure if this is the best thing that could have happened to me, or the worst.

"Maddie," I croak out.

"What *happened* to you?"

"I got my period."

"Oh. Is . . . is it your first time?"

"Yeah. It is."

Maddie says a word she doesn't say very much. Weirdly enough, that makes me feel a little better.

"Okay, okay. We can deal with this. I have pads in my bag," she says.

Huh. I didn't know she'd gotten her period. It must have happened while we were not talking. We used to know everything about each other. But right now I don't have time to feel sad about not knowing Maddie-things. I'm too busy freaking out about me-things. Still. I've been saved.

"Great!" I say. My voice wobbles.

"Uh . . . not great, actually. My bag is backstage."

Deep breaths. Maddie is helping me. I should not, not, not show any irritation toward her.

"Okay? So maybe you can, you know, get your bag."

That's about as nice as I can get when I have bloody underwear and a snot-covered face.

"Right!" Maddie says.

I hear shuffling noises. Then, Maddie says the bad word again. Uh-oh.

"What?" I ask. Even though I'm not sure I want to know.

"I think we're locked in," Maddie says.

I repeat the bad word.

Maddie squeaks. Okay, cursing isn't helping. I take a deep breath and try to pull myself together. "How are we locked in? Did you move the chair by the door?"

A long pause. "I . . . maybe? I was preoccupied, okay?"

Deep breaths. As much as I want to snap at Maddie—and I so, so do—I can't. I'm tired of fighting with her.

Anyway, it's not like getting mad will do anything to fix the problem.

I open my mouth to suggest that Maddie try to get someone's attention, but she's already marching over to the door.

"Hello!" she says. "We're locked in!"

"Louder," I tell her.

"I don't need help from the toilet, thanks," she says, and I can just imagine her glaring at me.

"That's too bad. I like to think of myself as a helpful toilet," I say. Might as well try a joke. It's not like panicking has accomplished anything here, and it's the kind of thing that makes Maddie laugh.

She giggles. It's loud and a bit hysterical, but still. It's something.

Maddie tries to get help again. "Hey! Can anyone hear me?"

Apparently, no one can. Maddie's footsteps clomp back toward my stall. "I think they're playing music or something," she says.

I stare into my red underwear. "So, we're trapped."

"Only for now," Maddie says. But she sounds about as hopeful as I feel. Which is not very.

A minute passes, then two. Maddie goes over to the door and yells again. It doesn't work. Big surprise. I sigh.

"Of all the people I could have ended up with . . ." Maddie mutters.

I bite down on the edge of my lip. I don't know whether she wanted me to hear that little comment or not, but either way I'm annoyed.

"I'm not exactly thrilled about this, either, you know," I say, in what probably is not my nicest voice. Whatever. I'm not in the mood for nice.

Another loooong pause.

"I know," Maddie says. "If . . . if it's worth anything, I really am sorry. For what I did."

Because I just can't help myself, I snort. "I'll bet you are."

"I mean it! I was just mad about the shoes, and I really needed help on my screenplay."

Uh, what? Are the bathroom fumes affecting Maddie's common sense or something? What does her screenplay have to do with anything? I glare at the bathroom door. Hard.

"So sorry," I say in my not-sorry voice. "But I don't actually care. About your shoes or your screenplay."

"That's fair, I guess."

Now she's not even arguing with me. At once, the anger leaves me. I sigh. If she's trying to be all mature and stuff here, I should make an effort, too. Besides, this so isn't really the time and place for drama.

"Let's be clear: What you did to me was really sucky," I say. "But I know I haven't always been the best friend to you, either."

A peace offering. I can only hope she sees it that way.

"I guess we were both crappy friends," she responds in a flat voice.

Well, I can't exactly disagree with that. But something about it just makes me mad. It's like Maddie has already given up on us.

183

And I don't want to do that. As mad as I was at her, as mad as I still am . . . I still want to be Maddie's friend. Maybe that makes me pathetic. I don't know.

"We . . . maybe we can try to do better?" I say.

"I think it's probably too late for that."

Thank goodness for the door to the bathroom stall. Maddie can't see me wince.

Another uncomfortable silence sets in, and all of a sudden I realize that Maddie hasn't gone to the bathroom yet. Despite the fact that there are two empty stalls. Then I remember how shaky her voice sounded when she first came in here and found me in my current super-pathetic state.

"Are you . . . are you okay, Mads?" I ask.

"What do you mean?"

Her voice is a bit cool. I can practically see her crossing her arms over her chest.

She wants me to back off, probably. But, well, we're stuck in a smelly bathroom. Besides, I can't help but think that maybe it'll be good for her to talk about whatever it is that's so obviously bothering her.

"I thought maybe you were upset about something. Since you came here and all. But you don't have to talk about it if you don't want to."

For the longest time, she doesn't respond. I probably messed up again. Just as I try to figure out how to fix things, she speaks.

"I'm too fat for the costumes. None of them fit me."

Whatever I'd been expecting her to say, it wasn't that. "Oh," I say. "You . . . you know . . ."

"Don't say I'm not fat!" Maddie interrupts.

"I wasn't going to say that!" I was, but now I won't. "I was just going to say that I can fix it. How about I go talk to Audrey and . . ."

"Stop!"

I scowl. "I was just trying to help!"

Maddie lets out a noise that is somewhere between a sigh and a shriek. "You always do this, Chloe! You always try to fix things. You try to fix *me*. I wasn't asking you to solve my problem. I was . . . oh, never mind. You wouldn't get it."

She's right. I don't.

"Anyway," Maddie says in her "so done talking about this" voice. "That doesn't matter right now. We kind of have more pressing problems."

"Like what?"

"Well, you may have noticed that we're currently locked in the bathroom."

Right. In the middle of our big heart-to-heart I kinda forgot about all that.

I chew on my lip. "I may have a solution."

CHAPTER NINETEEN

Maddie

My scowl widens more and more as Chloe explains her idea. I know she can't see me, but I glare at the bathroom stall door anyway.

"I am not climbing out the window," I say. "Nope. No way. Not even if you drag me out by the ankles."

"Please?"

It's just one word—one syllable, really—but it makes my skin prickle. How often have I heard Chloe say that word? *Please, Maddie. Do it for me. It's easy. It will be fun. I promise.*

I know very well what such promises are worth, and this time, I am not going to say yes. Even if Chloe does sound awfully close to hysterical, barricaded in her bathroom stall.

I take a deep breath. I have every intention of saying no. I have to. Still, maybe I could do a better job of explaining myself to her. "I'd like to help you," I say, my eyes fixed on the too-high bathroom window. "But . . . Chloe, I don't think I *can* climb out the window for you."

"Why not?"

Chloe sounds genuinely confused by this point, and I feel the strong desire to scream. But that will not solve a single one of our already-long list of problems. So I force myself to take a slow, steady breath before I speak.

"Chloe, you know I have dyspraxia. That means I'm not good at climbing things like you are. Just like I'm no good at dancing and don't tie my shoes the normal way. Or how I'm even bad at walking sometimes."

I expect her to argue with me, to tell me that no, I'm not *really* bad at those things, I just get in my own way. I've heard it from Chloe before, after all. I prepare counterarguments in my head and get ready to deploy them. But when Chloe finally speaks again, she does not contradict me.

"Okay. So . . . uh . . . so, what do we do?"

I hold back the angry, sarcastic response threatening to burst out of me. Chloe is listening to what I'm saying, I think, and that's new. Besides, given her current situation I can hardly blame her for being antsy.

"Do you think you can climb out the window?" I ask her.

"Probably, yeah. But I'm stuck here!"

I run a hand through my hair. "Maybe not."

"You found a pad?" Chloe asks hopefully.

"Uh, no. Sorry."

I proceed to teach her how to make a temporary pad out of toilet paper. It's a trick I figured out earlier this year when I didn't have any pads with me at school.

"That doesn't sound very comfortable," Chloe says once I'm done explaining.

"It's not."

She sighs. "Well, I guess being stuck in the bathroom isn't exactly comfortable, either."

A few minutes later, Chloe emerges from the stall. Her hair looks disheveled, and her eyes are puffy. Although I try

not to look at the big red stain on her white shorts, I can hardly avoid it.

Chloe blushes. "I know. It's gross."

I shrug. "It's biology." That's what Sandra told me right after I got my period.

"Well, biology is gross."

I can hardly argue with that.

Staring into the mirror, Chloe frowns at her reflection. "I don't feel any different," she says.

I don't know whether she's talking to herself or to me, but I respond anyway. "Why would you feel different?"

"I don't know, Maddie," she says, a bit snappishly. "It's just that everyone makes this out to be a huge deal. But I don't feel happy or grown-up or whatever. Just kind of blech, you know?"

"Do you want me to sing a song in your honor?"

"Oh, shut up," she says. But she's smiling, like she always used to do. I wish we could just stay here, in this moment where everything is more simple.

"So," I say. "Are you ready to get out of this place?"

Chloe pats down her hair to a mostly neat bob. "Yeah. Let's do it."

Even with her bloody shorts, she gives a determined grin. I cannot help but admire her composure. Chloe could be a character in a superhero movie for sure. Not like me. I try to push down the thought.

"If we're going to do this, we should use that one." I point to a window on the far side of the bathroom. "That way if we fall, we fall on grass, not dirt and rock."

Chloe gives me a loopy grin. "Good thing I have you to point this stuff out."

Together, we work to pull open the window. It's heavier than it looks, and I don't think I could have managed it without her. Once we've got it, Chloe leaps at least a foot into the air. She arches right through the window and lands on her feet, like an Olympic gymnast who just nailed her routine.

Brushing a bit of dirt off her clothes, Chloe grins widely. "Now it's your turn."

At that, my blood just about stops flowing through my veins. There is no way—absolutely no way at all—that I can do what Chloe just did. I just explained this to her. Why does she not understand?

"I can't," I tell her. I do not conceal my irritation.

"I know this is more difficult for you. I get it. Well, maybe I don't, not entirely. But I'll be right here to help you do it."

Folding my arms across my chest, I let out a deep breath. It is true that I do not want to be in this cramped bathroom for a single moment longer. And if Chloe is there to help me, well, maybe I can try. Maybe. It's just that the window is so high. And what if I get stuck? The humiliation I would face . . . I couldn't survive it, I know I couldn't.

"What if I get stuck?" I blurt out. "What if I embarrass myself again?"

"I'm here," she repeats.

She is here, smiling at me through the window in that way of hers. A real smile, the kind she only gives to a few people. Despite everything that happened, despite what I

did, I am still one of those people. And I start to think that maybe I should at least try to make the leap.

Adina would do it, I realize. Maybe . . . maybe I should try, too.

I unclench my fists. "Okay. I'll . . . I'll give it a try."

So I jump. I don't make it the first time. But I try again and again and again after that.

Finally, I make it to the window on attempt number four. Squeezing myself through the tiny window isn't easy as a not-tiny person, but I do it. The ground looks scarily far away, but Chloe extends her hand toward me. I grab it and leap down.

Somehow, unbelievably, I make it. Chloe flashes me a thumbs-up.

She totters on her feet, and before I fully recognize what's happening, she slips to the ground. A slew of curse words come out of her mouth.

My already fast heartbeat picks up its pace. Chloe is hurt, and it's my fault.

"Are you okay?" I ask.

Slowly, Chloe picks herself up. "Uh, yeah?" she says. But she does not sound particularly sure of herself on that point.

She takes a small step forward, favoring her left leg. I've been injured enough times to recognize a probable ankle sprain when I see one. This is bad. Beads of sweat start to form on my forehead, and I look around for help. There are some people way off in the distance, but I don't think I can yell loudly enough for them to hear.

Think, Maddie! Chloe needs me. So I offer her my shoulder to lean on.

"Do you think you can walk a little? I'll help?"

Chloe's face is still pinched and pale, and the stain still mars her shorts, more obvious than ever. But she nods. "Yeah."

Slowly, unsteadily, we start to walk. Together.

CHAPTER TWENTY

Chloe

As much as I so did not want to, I ended up spending the rest of the afternoon in the emergency room. The camp nurse wanted to make sure that my ankle wasn't actually broken. Lucky for me, it isn't. Unlucky for me, the ankle is sprained. It still kind of hurts when I put weight on it. I don't know how I'm supposed to be Galinda now. Audrey says we can work around it, but I have my doubts.

When I returned with a ginormous ankle brace and new clothes, a bunch of people came up to offer their sympathy. That's nice, I guess, but I can't help but wonder how many of them were calling me "Cramp Girl" two days ago.

I've been back for several hours when Maddie finally approaches me. Tonight's evening activity is a scavenger hunt. Which, needless to say, is not something I can do on a wobbly ankle. So I set myself up on an outside bench, with my ankle extended.

I scooch over for Maddie. She looks a bit unsure, but takes the seat. "Are you okay?" she asks.

Making a face, I shrug. "About as okay as I can be after spraining my ankle, I guess."

She nods. "Yeah. I've been there."

Now that she mentions it, Maddie has sprained her ankle

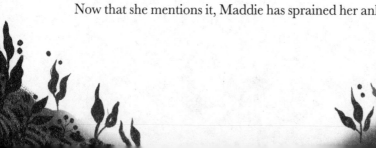

before. Multiple times, in fact. So I guess she would know all about this particular experience.

I want to say something to her. Thank her for saving me, maybe. But I don't know how to talk with Maddie anymore. After what happened today, are we friends again? I don't even know.

Maddie clears her throat, looking about as awkward as I feel. "Anyway. I just wanted to check to see that you're okay. With everything. Do you need any pads?"

I shake my head. The nurse took care of that, giving me more pads and tampons than I could possibly need. "I'm good with that," I tell Maddie, then pause. I want to say more, but I don't know if that's allowed. I continue anyway. "If you have any advice on how to deal with cramps, though, I'd love to hear it. Wow do they suck."

"Can't say I have any miracle cures, sorry." Her mouth twists into a half smile. "Maybe you could try Tortasil Relief."

That shouldn't be funny, after what Maddie did to me. But I giggle anyway. "I don't know if that stuff even works."

"After what you did for them, they should give you a lifetime supply," Maddie says. She fidgets with her hands. "I really am sorry about that, you know."

"I know. I'm sorry I was such a lousy friend before that."

Maddie smiles, but it's strained. "Well, all that's in the past now."

I try to smile back, but I can't. Yeah, I guess it is in the past. But if I've learned anything these last few months, it's that the past doesn't actually go away. It just kind of lurks

around, popping up when I least want or expect it to make an appearance. Poisoning everything.

I want to ask Maddie if we can be friends again now. Just as I try to find the right words, she mumbles something about the scavenger hunt and runs away.

About an hour into the activity, someone approaches me again. I smile when I see Sasha.

"Aren't you supposed to be scavenging or hunting or something?" I ask.

"I finished half the list. That's enough scavenging for me. Besides, I figured you were in need of some company over here."

Annoyingly, my heart skitters. I am, apparently, incapable of maintaining normal body functions when Sasha is around. It so does not help that the last time we saw each other, I had period shorts. Sasha is too nice to mention that, but still.

I smile at her. "Well, thanks."

I want to say more. Something about how I always appreciate Sasha's company, blah blah blah. But that's kind of sappy, and I'm not sure I'm ready for that.

If only I could know whether Sasha likes me. If she likes girls at all. I don't know the right way to ask. *Sasha, do you like girls?* seems way too direct. It's not fair. If she were a boy, I wouldn't have to ask. I could just assume.

"I might have to leave camp," Sasha says abruptly.

I stare at her. "What? Why?"

Sasha twirls a wavy strand of hair between her fingers. "It's . . . it's good news, maybe. I auditioned for a role before

194

camp—the lead part in a movie. I never thought I'd actually get it, but they invited a few people back for callbacks and . . . well, I don't know anything for sure. But I might get the part."

"That's amazing," I tell her, 100 percent sincere.

Maybe a few weeks ago I would have been overcome with jealousy. And, yeah, okay, even now I feel a twinge. But mostly, I'm just happy for her. She totally deserves good things. The part that gets me is the thing about her leaving camp.

"Why would you have to leave?" I ask.

"If they want to start production, I go."

She doesn't have to say anything more. That's just how it is.

It would be totally selfish of me to hope she doesn't get the part. Obviously. And I don't want that, really. I want her to be happy, and if she wants this part, then I want it, too.

Still . . . I just really want to spend the rest of camp with Sasha. Can't this movie change its production schedule a bit? I don't think that's too much to ask. Please, universe?

Sasha looks at me as if expecting something, and I realize I need to respond. I clear my throat.

"Well, I hope you get it. And . . . and I hope we can still do the musical together, too."

I look at her very carefully while I speak. Will she understand the things I mean but can't say? That it's not just about the musical, but her? The relationship we have?

Whatever that is.

She smiles at me, and her face looks so beautiful I almost want to look away. "I hope so, too."

195

CHAPTER
TWENTY-ONE

"So are we friends now?"

I glance up from my bowl of cereal to look at Chloe. She wears her usual face—the "I'm Chloe Winters and I'm in control of everything" face. But unless I am very much mistaken, she's straining to maintain it.

Pursing my lips, I consider how best to answer the question. The truth is, I think we are friends, too. Or at the very least, that we're not enemies anymore. The problem is, the more time I've had to think about yesterday, the more unsure I am about whether being friends with Chloe again is a good idea.

Sure, yesterday we had a moment. If life were a movie, that might be just the type of Heartwarming Moment that takes place right before the big climax. Best friends reunifying to take on the big enemy and all of that. But real life doesn't work like that. I just can't stop thinking about everything that came before—everything Chloe did to me, and everything I did to her.

Chloe and I are still stuck in the same script. I hurt her, she hurts me. She convinces me to do something utterly ridiculous, I follow her lead. It's like we're characters on a mediocre TV show that keeps getting renewed for some reason. Well, I want to be done with the whole drama.

"Sorry. But we're not friends," I tell her.

I don't look away while Chloe flinches. I owe her that much.

"But . . . you helped me. With the pad thing."

Chloe's cheeks flush faintly pink at the word *pad*, and I almost smile. Apparently there are some things that can penetrate her mask of utter coolness.

"You were facing a menstruation emergency. I would have helped anyone."

In all honesty, I'm not sure I would have followed just anyone out of a window. But that is kind of the problem, isn't it? Maybe things mostly worked out this time, but I should not be following Chloe out of windows. Following her script when I should be writing my own. Really, it's a miracle that it didn't end with both of us in full-leg casts.

Some people just shouldn't be friends.

Chloe sighs—so quiet I almost don't hear it. Then she nods. "Okay," she says. "If that's what you want."

I'm not sure that is what I want, really, but I can hardly tell that to Chloe. So I just give her a tight not-smile and return to my Rice Krispies. She takes the cue and leaves.

While I chew, I think. I think so much and so hard that I very nearly swallow my cereal the wrong way. That's yet another hazard of having dyspraxia. Things that are simple to everyone else aren't so simple for me, especially when I'm distracted. I cough and try to clear my throat.

My mind keeps turning back to everything that happened yesterday. On top of everything else, the awfulness with the too-small costumes still looms over me. If I am going to be in *Wicked*, then I need a costume that fits.

For maybe the first time ever, I arrive at rehearsal early. For definitely the first time ever, I approach Audrey.

"Maddie!" she greets me. Her purple-streaked hair is falling out of its bun.

I clear my throat. "Uh . . . hi. I, uh, wanted to talk to you. About a problem."

Inwardly I cringe at my own awkwardness. I knew there was a reason I didn't want to do this. Part of me wishes I'd asked Chloe to do it for me.

"I am here to solve problems," Audrey says. "What's going on?"

"It's, uh, the costumes. None of the robes fit me. They're . . . they're too small."

Although I want to whisper, I force myself to speak at a normal volume. I have nothing to be ashamed about, right? Even if it kind of feels like I do.

Audrey's smile vanishes, and she lets out a word that definitely qualifies as bad language. I flinch in response. This was a big, big mistake. I should have just dealt with the stupid, tight orange robe. What right do I have to ask for special treatment?

"Ack. Sorry, Maddie. I should explain." Audrey switches back to her Director Voice. "I am not mad at you, okay? I'm mad at myself. I should have done better by you."

Wow. Audrey is pretty cool for a grown-up, but I wasn't expecting her to say that.

"It was seriously uncool of me to not make sure that everyone has a costume that fits, and I am super sorry for that. The good news is, we can still fix it before showtime.

Now, how about you tell me what size you need, and I'll get you a fantabulous costume?"

"How?" I ask.

She blinks. "I'll order a new robe. Obviously! Do you want sequins? I think you'd look great with some sparkle."

Even though I'm not usually a sequins kind of a person, I nod. This has definitely gone better than I feared it would. And I did it all by myself, no help from Chloe required.

I allow my shoulders to relax, and while my mouth can't quite work itself into a smile, it loses some tension.

Maybe I'm still not thrilled about being in the musical, exactly, but at least I will have a great costume.

"I'm glad you came to me, Maddie," Audrey says. "I was actually going to run you down and ask you something."

Taking a big gulp, I resist the urge to run away. Is she going to ask me about my horrible dancing? Maybe she thinks it would be best if I'm just not in the musical at all. It would be easier, wouldn't it, for her to not have to bother with getting me a costume, and it's not like I'm any good. Just as I'm going through worst-case scenarios, Audrey says the last thing in the world I ever expected.

"I want you to learn Elphaba's part. As an understudy."
What?

I must say that out loud, because Audrey repeats herself. "Look, I know it isn't the most glamorous thing in the world, but understudies are important for any production. I've thought about this, and you're the actor for the job."

I'm not an actor at all! Or at least, I shouldn't be an actor. Doesn't Audrey know what happened the last time I tried

to perform for real? And now she's asking me to play the lead—not just the lead, but the title character. The wicked witch.

Despite the rapidly growing lump in my chest, I try to keep my breaths steady. Maybe I can still convince Audrey this is a terrible idea. Theoretically that shouldn't be difficult because it is a terrible idea. Horrendous. The worst.

"I . . . I really don't think I'm the right person," I say.

"Well, I disagree. You're a talented singer and actor. I know you can memorize lines because I've seen you mouthing the words to the songs. Your vocal range is right for the part. If you had to fill in for Sasha, I am sure you would do a fantastic job."

I can't help but feel a little taken in by all her praise. But it does little to squash the terror.

"I . . . I don't know," I say weakly. "If I'm so great, why didn't you give me a better part in the first place?"

Audrey raises an eyebrow. "I didn't think you wanted one. But now we need you. If for any reason Sasha can't perform, can you be our Elphaba?"

I should say no. Sorry, but can't you find someone else? I don't want this, not after *The Music Man.*

Yes, you do want it, whispers a voice in my head. A very Chloe-like voice. *Come on, Maddie. Take a risk. Jump out the window with me.*

I'll fall, I argue with Chloe in my head.

Then I'll be there to catch you, Chloe responds.

I don't believe you.

Audrey stares at me, waiting for my answer.

Adina would say yes. Any superhero would. But I'm not exactly superhero material, am I?

I open my mouth to say no.

"Yes. I'll do it."

CHAPTER TWENTY-TWO

Chloe

The rest of the week goes the same as it always does. Maddie ignores me. Sasha talks to me, but I never manage to say any of the really important stuff. We rehearse the play. Rinse and repeat.

Today Sasha isn't at lunch, so I eat alone. I don't care. Really, I don't. Except for the fact that I do.

Maddie eats alone, too. For a moment, we make eye contact. She carries a tray of food and I sip from my lemonade. In that moment I think maybe she'll come over and sit next to me. Like she always did at school. But she turns away and shuffles toward the opposite end of the room.

Yeah, okay. I get it. She doesn't want to be friends. I don't get why, but whatever.

Stupid of me to ever think that things between us could be good again.

Anyway. Where is Sasha? Is she taking a nap or something? That doesn't sound like something she'd do, but I like it better than any other explanation.

When I arrive at afternoon rehearsal, she's still nowhere to be found. I remember what she said about auditioning for a movie, and my stomach twists.

"Where's Sasha?" I ask Audrey the moment I see her.

For the first time since I've known her, Audrey seems

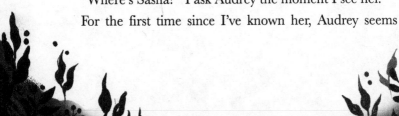

frazzled. Her forehead wrinkles look like they're about to pop off her face.

"About that," she says. "I don't want anyone to freak out, but . . . I'm afraid we have a bit of a problem. Sasha has to leave camp."

Audrey goes on about the musical and understudies and a bunch of other stuff that I don't care about. Not now.

"Why is she leaving?" I interrupt. "Did she get that part in the movie?"

"Yes. Which is great for her, I know, but it does present us with something of a pickle."

Audrey glares at her clipboard as though it were personally responsible for Sasha leaving.

"Is she . . . has she left yet?" I ask.

What I think but do not say is: *Did she leave without seeing me? Without saying goodbye?*

"No, she's packing and then her parents are coming by. I think—"

But I don't hear what Audrey thinks. I sprint out of the barn.

When I arrive back at the cabin, Sasha is hunched over her trunk. Her clothes are spread out over the bed. To my surprise, I recognize a bunch of them. I smile at the green apple–patterned dress, which I remember from the day we met. I see the checkered shorts and think back to the time we had frozen yogurt. And on the day she comforted me, after Maddie did what she did, she was wearing that shirt with red and purple flowers. Now she's throwing it all in the trunk.

203

"Chloe?"

I put my hands in my pockets. "Hi," I say.

Suddenly my tongue feels heavy. I don't want to think about it, but this could be the last time I see Sasha. Ever. And if it is, well, I have to make it count.

She smiles at me with crinkled eyes. "I guess you heard I'm leaving."

"Yeah. You're going to be a movie star now."

Sasha blushes. "Maybe."

"You'll do great. I know it," I tell her.

As I speak, I search myself for pangs of jealousy. I don't find any. I'm happy for her. I just wish she didn't have to leave.

Sasha turns toward me. "Chloe, when you were on TV, were you ever scared?"

"All the time."

It's the truth, but I've never told anyone else before. Chloe Winters isn't supposed to get stage fright.

"Oh," she says. "Does it ever get better?"

"Yeah. But it never really goes away."

Sasha nods, apparently satisfied with my answer. She looks at her trunk and sighs. "I really do wish I could have done *Wicked* with you."

"Me too."

For the next several minutes, Sasha continues packing. Neither of us says anything. There is so much I want to say, I barely know where to begin. Should I tell her how I feel? I want to, but . . . what if she doesn't feel the same way? I don't mean to be dramatic or whatever, but I couldn't take that.

I decide to start small. "Can we be friends after camp?"

Her eyebrows rise. "Definitely. I think friends are forever, no matter if we're in camp or not."

It's a sweet answer. But of course I know that friends aren't forever. Not always. And anyway, I don't just want to be Sasha's friend.

"You live in West Hollywood, right?" I ask.

"Yeah."

"That's not so far from me in Pasadena." I take a deep breath and try to gather up some nerve. "Maybe we could, I don't know, meet up or something."

"Oh, definitely."

Am I imagining the note of enthusiasm in her voice? No. I don't think so. The problem is, I still haven't said the thing I really want to say. The thing I have to say, before it's too late.

Come on, a voice in my head says. It's softer than my usual head voices. Sweeter, too. Almost like Maddie's voice. *You can do this. Just be honest.*

I draw in a huge breath. "Um. Okay. I just wanted to know . . ."

Get on with it, Chloe!

"I wanted to know if maybe you wanted to be . . . not just friends. I mean, not that being friends is bad. Friends are good!" I'm babbling. Time for the point. "But I thought maybe we could be, like, romantic friends?"

Her eyes widen. "You like girls?"

"Yes," I say. "I like girls. And . . . I especially like you."

"Well, I like you, too, Chloe."

205

The smile she gives me in return makes my insides burst. Oh. Em. Gee.

She likes me. She really likes me.

Just as I'm starting to process this beautiful, wonderful news, she leans forward and kisses me. On the mouth.

This is nothing like kissing Carlos. Nothing at all. We pull apart pretty quickly, and both of us are grinning. In fact, I'm pretty sure I'll never stop smiling.

I try to come up with the perfect thing to say after a first-kiss-for-real. Before I can figure it out, Hannah bursts into the room.

"Sasha, your parents are here."

Sasha makes a face. "I guess that's my cue to go."

Even though I'm still in a state of post-kiss happiness, my throat tightens a bit. "I guess this is goodbye, then."

"Goodbye for now," she corrects.

"Right."

She gives me a wink before she starts dragging her trunk across the cabin. As she walks away, I can still feel my skin buzzing.

While I walk back to rehearsal, I start belting "Dancing Through Life" at top volume. I don't care if anyone hears me. Let them hear. Cheesy as it sounds, I do feel like I'm dancing through life.

Right now, I can almost forget that with Sasha gone, I have no friends.

CHAPTER TWENTY-THREE

Maddie

I arrive at rehearsal a little late. No one much cares if a side character is missing, after all. Unfortunately, the barn has descended into a state of panic. Within the space of a minute, I hear at least three people proclaim that we are "totally doomed!!!"

Goodness knows that theater kids have a flair for the dramatic, but they sure sound like they mean it. Looking around at the throngs of campers, I frown. We still have six days until the musical. I didn't expect this level of chaos until dress rehearsal. What could have possibly happened?

"People!" Audrey says in full director volume. "I have a proposition. How about we all stop panicking for five minutes so we can discuss the situation? Once we've talked, I give you my full permission to panic as much as you like."

"What if we say no?" someone calls from the crowd.

Audrey gives a full-mouthed smile. "Yeah, so that option isn't actually on the table. So! I guess all of you have heard by now that Sasha will not be able to perform with us."

I gulp. Maybe everyone else heard, but this is the first I've heard of it. I break into a sweat. She isn't actually going to ask me to step in for Sasha, is she?

Knowing what I know about Audrey, that seems like a definite possibility. I try to keep my breath steady as I listen.

"Obviously, this sucks," Audrey says bluntly. "I'm not going to sugarcoat it. But we in show business always say that the show must go on, and so it will."

"How?" Mara asks. She sounds almost too eager.

"Glad you asked! It's actually very simple. We need an Elphaba."

Even though Audrey does not look directly at me, I feel the weight of her gaze anyway. I try not to shrink myself, even though I would love nothing more than to disappear into a puddle, just like Elphaba at the end of the musical.

But another, possibly bigger part of me, wants this. I want it a whole lot.

I might fall in front of everyone, again. And yet . . .

I raise my hand. "I've been working on the part," I say.

Ever since my conversation with Audrey, I've been studying the playbook, trying to memorize lines and cues. I'm pretty confident that I have most of Elphaba's part committed to memory. Of course, I can't say I'm confident about literally anything else.

Audrey beams at me. "Great news! Can you be our Elphaba, Maddie?"

Studying the lines in my palm, I pause before I answer. "Well, I definitely won't be as good as Sasha. I think we all know that. But I do know the lines."

"Don't sell yourself short," Audrey says. "If you know the lines, you're already doing great."

That's when Chloe speaks up. "Maddie's going to be fantastic."

As usual, Chloe is so very sure of herself. But also she's

sure of *me*, as though the whole disaster of *The Music Man* never happened at all.

"I can probably do the singing and acting," I say, even though I am not sure of any such thing. "But there's kind of a big problem. I can't dance. There's this disability, it's called dyspraxia and I have it . . . but anyway, I can't dance. Everyone knows it."

My face flushes pink while I speak. I don't like talking about dyspraxia with anyone other than my moms. Will Audrey ask a bunch of ridiculous questions, or simply pooh-pooh what I said outright? It may not seem very Audrey-like, but people get funny when you say you have a disability. I've had plenty of perfectly nice teachers tell me that I must be wrong, that I don't *really* have dyspraxia at all.

Plus, all the other kids are staring at me. No one says anything mean, but I don't trust them even a little bit.

Audrey continues playing with her pen and nods. "That's helpful for me to know, thanks. But as your director, I really do believe that your dancing abilities may not matter as much as you think. The character of Elphaba is awkward and unsure of herself. You don't need to be a brilliant dancer to inhabit the role."

Okay, she has a point. But I still can't quite believe that my dancing doesn't matter. After all, Mrs. Paroo wasn't supposed to be a hard part, yet I managed to mess that one up in spectacular fashion.

"I still don't know if I can do all the choreography. And the costumes . . . Sasha and I aren't the same size . . ."

My cheeks are on fire when I talk about the costumes.

Part of me expects someone to snicker and make some sort of snide comment about how Elphaba can't be fat. Because obviously.

It doesn't happen, though, and I start to think that maybe Elphaba can be fat—that fat girls can be the stars of our own stories.

"We can make adjustments to choreography and to costumes," Audrey says. She has resumed all of her directorial firmness.

Chloe turns to me. "I'll help."

I don't know if I believe her, but I very much want to. I want to believe that Chloe will be there for me throughout the whole thing, standing by me through every song and giving me the reassurances I so desperately need. I want to believe that very much.

Taking a steady breath, I speak again. "Okay. I . . . I guess I'll do it."

Audrey claps her hands together in applause. "Maddie, you're a lifesaver. The show will go on!"

The rest of the cast breaks out clapping, too. Even Mara. Which feels good, I guess, but I haven't done anything yet. I can only hope they'll still be clapping at the end of the show.

The rest of the day passes in a blur as Audrey and Chloe try to turn me into a passable Elphaba. I know all the words to the songs, thanks to Chloe's *Wicked* obsession, but there's so much else I need to learn. So many turns and pauses and exits and entrances. I wish I could write it down on my hands to keep everything straight, but there isn't enough room for it all.

Chloe tries to be patient with me, but she's still Chloe.

I let out a pained sigh after I mess up the stage directions during "Defying Gravity" for the fifth time.

"Stage left is that way, you know." She points.

Anger bubbles up inside my chest, and I don't bother trying to suppress it. "I do know that, actually!"

I'm maybe a little loud, and Chloe flinches. "Okay, okay. I was just trying to help."

"Well, you weren't helping. At all."

Her face twists with annoyance. "*Well*, Maddie, maybe if you would tell me what you need for once, I could do better."

I want to respond right away, but I don't. As much as I don't want to say so, I have to at least consider the possibility that Chloe has a point. It is true that I don't often tell her what I need.

But I shouldn't have to! She should just know, shouldn't she?

Before I can come up with a clever response, Audrey interrupts. "Ooookay. Let's take a break. Maybe after some time cooling off, you can put aside your personal conflict and start being actors again."

Both of us flush with embarrassment. For the rest of the day, neither of us says anything to the other. The entire time, one thought keeps running through my mind. How, how, *how* am I going to do this?

CHAPTER TWENTY-FOUR

Chloe

Three days. Seventy-two hours. I don't know how many minutes, but it doesn't matter. In three days, we will be performing *Wicked*.

And yeah, maybe it is just a camp musical. But it's a performance and I'm in it and everything has to go well. Especially since Maddie is now my costar.

Maddie said we're not friends. Still, I can't help but think that maybe she'll change her mind. Or maybe I just hope.

After the disastrous first day, I haven't given Maddie any advice. She's made it clear that she doesn't want my help. I can't quite shake the feeling there's something else she wants from me, though. She won't actually tell me what it is, because that would just be too easy. Or something.

I decide to try a compliment.

"You're doing better with dancing," I tell Maddie after we finish up morning rehearsal.

She glares at me. As if I just insulted her, which I totally did not.

"I'm still not good."

Ugh, this is just awkward. "You're fine! Most people don't know the difference between okay dancing and good dancing."

Maddie won't tolerate hearing anything that isn't 100

percent true. But what I said *is* true. Seriously, our audience is going to be parents and stuff. They won't notice if Maddie fumbles a few steps. Even Audrey said so the other day.

Biting on her lip, Maddie seems to consider what I said. Then she sighs. "They'll know what good dancing looks like when I'm standing right next to *you*."

I bite back a mean response. "I have a bad ankle, in case you haven't noticed! My dancing isn't exactly brilliant."

"You're still better than me."

Sighing, I try not to grit my teeth.

"Is it really so important for you to be better than me at dancing?"

Maddie's jaw clenches so tight I think maybe she'll never speak again. When she does, her voice is made of steel.

"I think it's safe to say that I'll never be better than you at much of anything."

I wince. Now I wish I'd just kept my big stupid mouth shut. But now I'm in this conversation, for better or worse. (Definitely worse.)

"You're better than me at loads of things. Like writing."

Maddie shakes her head. "Doesn't count."

Sighing, I press my fingers to my forehead. "Uh, why not? Writing is kind of important."

I probably sound snide. I don't mean to! Maddie is just frustrating me. A lot.

She makes another face and shrugs. "No one cares about writing except for teachers. You . . . you're . . ."

Her voice trails off. I clench my fists.

"I'm what?" I ask.

Maddie makes a grunt-y noise. "You're you! You're pretty and talented and . . . and *thin*. When you're onstage, everyone watches and listens and applauds your . . . your Chloeness. How am I supposed to stand next to you and sing?"

Is she *jealous* of me? The thought seems ridiculous . . . but there is no other explanation.

"It's not always so great, being pretty and talented and all that," I say in a quiet voice.

Maddie shrugs. "Maybe. But it's definitely not great not being any of those things, either."

And there is absolutely nothing I can say to that.

For the next three days, Maddie and I exist as though we live in one of Galinda's mechanical bubble thingies. We are constantly together, rehearsing. Yet we aren't really *together*. Whenever a scene ends, an uncomfortable silence falls.

Maddie is a good Elphaba. Maybe she isn't Sasha, and yeah, okay, her dancing isn't great, but it works for the part. I think we make a pretty good team onstage, as Elphie and Galinda. If only we could have a conversation as Maddie and Chloe.

I keep thinking about what Maddie told me, and the more I think about it, the more confused I get. Like, okay, Maddie is jealous of me. But what on Earth am I supposed to do with that? I can't stop being me!

Maybe Maddie is right. Maybe we shouldn't be friends.

Between the constant annoyance of Maddie-related thoughts and rehearsals, I almost forget that musical day isn't just our big performance. It's also the last day of camp.

My mother will be here. That brings up a whole new set of worries.

On the morning of the musical, I wake up early. Sleep is hard when I have so much to think about. I settle on my bed with my phone and cue up the Wicked soundtrack. I want to slip into being Galinda.

But I can't stop being Chloe. Not really. I don't know what I'm going to say to Cordelia when I see her. So much has happened this last month, and I don't know how to talk to her about any of it.

I'm so busy thinking that I almost don't notice Maddie slinking up to my bed. When it finally registers, I yank out my headphones.

"Hi," I tell her.

"Uh, hi," she says.

Even though she was the one to approach me, she looks awkward and uncertain. I raise my eyebrows, and she smiles a bit sheepishly.

"I know we, um, haven't really been getting along, but you seemed kind of down, so I thought I'd check in on you."

I hold back one of my meaner responses. We're not friends, according to Maddie, so why would she bother to check in on me? It's a legit question, in my opinion. But it's also true that she's being kind to me. Even though she doesn't have to do that.

I fiddle with my blanket. "Just nervous about today, I guess."

Maddie narrows her eyes. "You're nervous for the performance? Really?"

"No," I admit. "For seeing my mother."

"Ah," Maddie says.

She doesn't say anything else. But she also doesn't move to leave. I choose to interpret this as her being open to listening to me talk about my feelings or whatever.

You know. Like friends do.

And yeah, maybe I'm not usually the talk-about-feelings-and-weep type, but I've just had so many feelings inside me for so long and I haven't been able to talk about any of them. Not since Sasha left six days ago.

Maddie says we're not friends anymore. But she's here, acting like a friend. So I might as well go for it.

"I like girls," I say.

Maddie turns toward me. Her mouth falls open a bit, but she quickly puts her face back to normal-ish. "You mean romantically?"

"Yes."

Other than Sasha, Maddie is the first person I've ever told. Because of course she would be. She smiles at me. It's a strange sight these days, but a welcome one.

"That's cool. We can talk about it. Or not. Whatever you want."

"Sasha and I kissed," I say before I can back out of it. "Before she left."

Maddie claps her hands together. Right now she looks an awful lot like a best friend. Like *my* best friend. "Oooh! That's so great!"

"I think so," I tell her.

216

"You know, I don't think we've ever talked about one of your crushes before," Maddie says.

We most definitely have not. "I guess I didn't want to admit to you that I'm gay. I couldn't even admit it to myself for the longest time."

"Well, I'm glad you did," Maddie says.

"I don't know if I can tell Cordelia. At least, not now."

For a long moment, Maddie just looks at me. "You don't have to if you don't want to," she says, her voice kinder than I've heard it in ages.

Somehow, Maddie still knows the exact right thing to say. Even though we're not friends, not anymore, I reach out and squeeze her hand. She squeezes back. And all of a sudden, I get it. Maybe . . . maybe *this* is what Maddie needs from me. Not someone to give her advice and tell her what to do and make mean little remarks. Maybe what she needs is someone to just listen while she vents about whatever.

Someone like Maddie.

Maddie

The green makeup makes me feel like my face has doubled in weight. A million worries race through my brain. Will the face paint crack? Will I forget my lines? Will I trip and humiliate myself, again?

On the bright side, my black robe fits perfectly. If I have to dance, at least I have a costume that doesn't itch or squash my boobs. That alone makes things better than my last performance.

Just like last time, Chloe stands next to me. She does a few yoga-type poses for her usual pre-performance routine. I just try not to touch my face.

"Hey," she says softly. "Are you okay?"

I force a laugh. "Does it matter if I'm not?"

"Of course it does!"

The fierceness in her voice takes me by surprise, I guess. I stare at her.

"Anyway," she says. "I know this is scary for you. But I'm here. If you want to talk. Or whatever."

"Is freaking out an option?"

Chloe laughs. "If you want it to be."

She reaches over and pats me on the shoulder. The weight of her hand, so familiar yet so new, grounds me. Maybe I can do this.

"What if I fall again?" I blurt out.

She takes her time before responding. "Look at it this way. You've already had one, um, problem onstage this year. What are the odds it will happen again?"

"To me? Pretty good."

Chloe chews on her pink lips. "Then you'll get through it, Maddie. You got through it before and you can do it again."

I shift from one foot to the other. I want to tell her she's wrong, she can't possibly understand, et cetera et cetera.

Except I'm not sure that she is wrong. As horrible and awful and humiliating as the whole *Music Man* thing was, I survived it. Just like I survived a month at camp when everything that could go wrong did go wrong.

I really, really hope that I don't fall again—but if I do, I will survive. I've done it before.

"Huh. I guess you're right."

Chloe gives me her real smile. "I usually am," she says, but not in a way that's super annoying.

I want to say more, to thank her maybe, but before I can find the words Audrey's voice rings through the backstage area. "Opening places! It's almost showtime, folks."

Heart hammering in my throat, I wait for the show to begin.

Most of act 1 passes by in a not-quite-real blur. I say my lines and sing without too much trouble. I stumble through the dancing more times than I'd prefer, but I try not to let it bother me. I remember what Audrey said, about how Elphaba is supposed to be awkward. It helps, at least a little.

219

Soon enough, the big moment arrives.

Out of everything I do as Elphaba, the absolute scariest part is singing "Defying Gravity." It's a song for a great singer, and I am not one. Besides, everyone at camp heard Chloe sing the song that first night here. The way the song is supposed to be, with all of Chloe's power and flourishes.

I made the mistake of mentioning this during rehearsal one time. Audrey just shook her head at me. "Don't sing it like Chloe," she said. "Sing it like Maddie playing Elphaba. Think about the song. Think about what it means to you and to Elphaba."

Even now, it all feels so impossible. But I try anyway. I do what Audrey told me and I think about the song.

For her entire life, Elphaba has never been good enough. She went to Shiz hoping to find glory, but really it was just more people being jerks to her. I can understand that. But then, she makes it to Oz, and she learns how to fly.

As a girl who can't even walk straight half the time, I can't exactly relate. But I guess that's what being an actor is all about.

And, yes, maybe I'm not Chloe. Still, I am here and I am Elphaba and I am going to do this.

The big part of the song doesn't come right away. First, Chloe and I must do the lead-up scene.

"Don't be afraid," Chloe tells me.

I know it isn't really Chloe speaking to me. She's just saying Galinda's line. The words give me a bit of comfort anyway.

"I'm not afraid," I say—another line. I try to sound like

I believe it. Maybe I really will. "It's the wizard who should be afraid of me."

Chloe and I go through the rest of the dialogue, arguing with each other. Soon it is my time to really and truly sing. I draw in a deep breath before I begin. I will need every bit of air to land these notes.

I begin. "Something has changed within me. Something is not the same."

My voice cracks. Not a lot, maybe not enough for most people to notice. But it does and I cringe. Next to me, Chloe holds my hand. This isn't part of the script, but she does it anyway. For me?

I am doing this.

Chloe puts a cloak on me, exactly like we rehearsed. She squeezes my shoulder while she does it and I just barely stop myself from smiling at her. "Defying Gravity" isn't really a smiley song.

As the song continues, we move closer together. She puts her arm around my shoulders and I do the same. The music swells into a crescendo, and between that and my heartbeat it's a miracle that I can hear anything at all.

I sway on my feet, balance tottering.

Oh. Oh no. It is happening again.

But just as I prepare myself for the fall, Chloe's grip around me tightens. She holds me up, saving me from near-certain embarrassment.

I look at her. *Thank you*, I say to her with my eyes. *Thank you, thank you, thank you.*

221

Somewhere in the back of my mind, I note that Chloe was right. I stumbled, sure, but then I survived it.

I can do this.

Together, we sing: "I hope you're happy, in the end. I hope you're happy, my friend."

Moments later, guards rush on the stage to split us up, yanking Chloe—well, Galinda—away from me. I am standing alone onstage.

All eyes are on me, and maybe right now I should care about the size of my body or whether my posture is awkward. But in the awesomeness of the moment, I find that I don't care much at all. I am Elphaba—a fat Elphaba who has dyspraxia—and I am the star of the show.

I sing. I sing with more power and flourish than I ever knew I possessed. And when the final verse comes, I want to relish the moment.

". . . no wizard that there is or was is ever gonna bring me dooooown," I conclude.

In my side vision, I can see Chloe beaming offstage as she watches me. When the curtain falls on the first act, I'm beaming too.

And for the first time in a long time, I am overcome with the desire to capture this moment in a screenplay.

CHAPTER TWENTY-SIX

Chloe

Being Galinda puts me in a happy trance. I act, dance, and sing through joy, heartbreak, and betrayal. I do a pretty great job, if I do say so myself. The audience practically roars for Maddie and me at the end of our last number.

But the musical ends, as it must. I'm Chloe again. With all the usual sucky-ness and confusion. Ugh.

I don't like it. Still, I only have a few hours left at camp. I guess I should do what I can to deal with stuff.

First up on my to-do list: Talk to my mother.

The moment I take my final bow, she's there to greet me backstage. She beams at me. Gah, I think I actually missed her. I didn't expect that, but I did.

"You were brilliant, darling," she tells me.

Cordelia's voice lacks even a hint of fakeness, and I feel warm all over. I know musicals aren't really her thing and anyway, I wasn't brilliant. Good, maybe, but hardly spectacular. Still, she's glowing at me as if I just won the Tony.

"Now! You have to tell me all about your summer. How was camp? Did you make any new friends? You didn't get a sunburn, did you?"

She fluffs my hair. Even though I'm too old for that, I kind of like it anyway. I try to get my thoughts together.

"Camp was great," I say.

That part is definitely true. Of course, I don't know the right words to say that camp was great and I'm a lesbian and I kissed a girl and, oh yeah, I also got my period for the first time. There will be time for that later. Once I figure out how I want to do it. For now, I just want to enjoy seeing my mom for the first time in a month.

"I'm thrilled to hear it, darling," she says. "So I suppose you have your sights set on Broadway now, yes?"

Before I answer, I chew my lip. Because yeah, of course I want to end up on Broadway someday. Problem is, I'm not sure that's what Cordelia is asking. Cordelia being Cordelia and all.

"Yeah. I want that. Someday."

She nods. "Okay. Excellent. We can add musicals to your repertoire and let your agent know. Maybe we can even visit New York, really get a sense of the Broadway scene. I'm sure there are audition opportunities—"

"No," I say. My voice rings out, as if I'm still onstage projecting to the last row. "I want to do Broadway when I'm grown-up. Now . . . now I just want to be a kid. No more auditions. Not for movies or commercials or anything."

I can't believe I just said that. But I did, and even though my mom is staring at me with her mouth dangling open, I feel pretty freaking great.

"But sweetie," Cordelia says. "You're so good at per-forming. You can be a star. I know you can."

Clenching my fists, I resist the urge to yell. Or to give in. Both options have some appeal.

"I'd rather do eighth grade. Like a normal kid, you know? I want to do the school musical again. And go back to camp next year. That would be so great. I can't do that if I have a million auditions and stuff."

Cordelia keeps looking at me. But she doesn't say no.

"You've changed in the last four weeks, haven't you?" she remarks finally.

She has no idea how much, but she will. I smile.

"Yes," I say. "Yes, I have."

Twiddling my fingers, I look up at her. I've done my part. Now I just have to wait for her answer.

"Honey, if you don't want to do auditions this year, then we won't," she says.

I squeal. I look ridiculous, probably, but I do it anyway. She listened to me! She really listened to me.

That's one item on my to-do list checked off. Now for thing number two: Talk to Maddie.

CHAPTER
TWENTY-SEVEN

Maddie

After the terrifying wonderfulness of the musical, packing up my stuff is just boring. But with help from my moms, I manage it. They tell me how proud they are at least once every five minutes. I can't say I mind that much.

Finally, I'm fully packed. Sandra and I drag my trunk over to the main entrance while Mom circles by with the car.

I didn't plan it, but of course I've ended up mere feet away from Chloe and her superchic bags. The script of the universe always plops me into the same scene as Chloe. She looks at me, and Sandra not-so-subtly drifts away from us. Whether I like it or not, we are going to talk.

"Some summer, right?" she says.

"Yeah."

Neither of us says anything else. But it's a comfortable sort of quiet, not one of those anxiety-provoking "will you just say something before I have to" moments.

I am the one to break the silence. "So. What comes next?"

Chloe looks down at a suitcase handle.

"Next we go back to real life," she says. A slight sigh punctuates her words.

I know what she means—homework, parents, all the middle school problems. For her, there will probably be auditions

and all the other stuff that come with being an actor. But one ginormous question remains.

"What's going to happen to us?" I ask.

"What do you want for us?" she responds.

Even though I don't think it's very fair to answer a question with another question, I consider it.

Because the truth of the matter is that I don't know what I want to happen when it comes to Chloe and me. Okay, I definitely do not want things to go back the way they were before, with both of us pretending that the other didn't exist. Still, do I want a return to the before-before, when we were best friends? Is that even possible anymore?

Part of me—maybe a lot of me—wants to be Chloe's best friend again. I'm familiar with that part. It's comfortable. Besides, there are loads of wonderful things about being Chloe's friend. When I'm her friend, the screenplay of my life is usually more exciting, more fun, more everything.

The problem is, I know being Chloe's friend isn't just sleepovers and movies and notes passed during science class. At some point, she might hurt me, or I might hurt her. It wouldn't be the first time.

"I just . . . I don't want us to hurt each other again," I say at last.

Chloe nods. "I don't want that, either. Believe me."

I believe her, but what if we can't ever stop being horrible to each other? As though we're characters in a TV show, never changing, never moving.

"What happens if we get into another fight? Something worse?"

Although Chloe looks like she's dying to respond, she doesn't. Not right away. She keeps chewing on her lip. Then, she speaks.

"I get that. There are no guarantees. So I guess I'm asking you to take a risk."

After everything that happened this summer, I understand risk. I mean, I thought I could never do another musical after The Incident. But I survived, with a little help from Chloe. I even, dare I say, did well. I changed the script.

It occurs to me all of a sudden that I am the writer of my own screenplay. I don't have to be a static character, trapped in anger and resentment of things that happened before. My story is just that—*mine*.

"I'd like to try being your friend," I tell Chloe. "But if we're going to do this, you need to act like my friend. When I need support and sympathy and stuff, you can't go into fix-Maddie mode like you did before. I need you to be like . . . like you were today. You know, *kind*."

My face flushes a little as I speak, because talking about kindness and friendship and stuff is a bit embarrassing. Still, I needed to say it.

Chloe nods. "I get that. I want to be that kind of friend for you. But I need a few things from you, too."

I suppose that's fair enough. "What?"

"I need you to actually tell me what you need. You know, like you just did."

She smiles at me, and I smile back. Then she continues. "And also . . . can you maybe, I don't know, not be jealous of me?"

I squirm.

"I can't promise that I'll never, ever get jealous again," I admit. "But I'll give it my best shot."

She reaches out and squeezes my shoulder. "So. Friends again?"

"Yeah. Let's try."

If we were still little kids, this would turn into a whole big dramatic scene. I would declare that Chloe and I are destined to be friends forever and ever. She would agree, and we'd make up a secret handshake and give each other special bracelets.

Of course I don't do anything like that, and neither does she. I guess we both realize that forever is an awfully long time. There's no telling what might happen between now and forever. Or even what might happen this month.

The truth is, Chloe and I might not be best friends forever. That's just reality. But we'll always be once-best friends, if that's the right term for it. We'll always be connected, even if only through the past. My own personal backstory.

Maybe that should make me sad, but it doesn't. Mostly I feel like things are finally right. If I had my notebook right now, I could start scribbling down the best, most amazing story.

I realize now that Adina doesn't really want to attack anyone with magical snakes. Golems, after all, aren't so different from people. Adina wants—she *needs*—a true friend, someone who loves and accepts her for who she is. Even after all the missteps and mistakes.

Maybe the world doesn't always love and accept a golem

girl, but Adina can be loved, and she can love herself. She can tell her friends what she needs. She can make things just a little bit better, one day at a time. She can be a friend.

Later, I'll start writing it all down.

As I'm having my Moment of Introspection, Mom's car pulls up. (She never respects my Moments of Introspection, does she?)

I reach for my trunk. "So . . . see you around," I tell Chloe.

"You know it."

Sandra helps me with the trunk, and soon I'm sitting in the backseat while the engine thrums to life. I watch the WELCOME TO CAMP ROSEWOOD sign fade into the distance, becoming nothing more than a small brown dot on the landscape.

If my life were a movie, we would be moving into the closing credits right about now. Of course real life doesn't work like that. This isn't the end of anything.

Now I get to write what comes next.

ACKNOWLEDGMENTS

Somehow, writing a book never really gets easier. I am so fortunate to have a wonderful team behind me that helped me pull this one together.

Much thanks to my editor, Dana Chidiac. As always, your insightful questions and comments have helped me to find the heart of the book and show these characters to the world. I'm so glad we got to work together on Maddie and Chloe's story.

Sofia Miller brought Maddie and Chloe to life with her breathtaking illustration, and Mallory Grigg designed a cover that makes me smile every time I see it. Huge thanks to both of you!

Thanks also to the rest of the team at Macmillan and Henry Holt Books for Young Readers: Ann Marie Wong, Jean Feiwel, Valery Badio, Alexei Esikoff, Kristen Stedman, Mariel Dawson, Melissa Zar, Molly Ellis, Mary Van Akin, Jen Edwards, and everyone else who has worked on sales, marketing, publicity, and school/library outreach.

Next, a huge thanks to my agent, Jennifer Laughran. Your hard work, savvy, and honesty make navigating this business so much easier and less stressful. Thanks to TJ Ohler, Bex Livermore, Alison Nolen, and the rest of the team at Andrea Brown Literary Agency for all the work you do for authors.

Many writers took a look at this book in various stages and provided helpful feedback. Thank you to Eric Bell, Jennifer Brown, Jess Creaden, Adrianna Cuevas, Maria Frazer, and Meera Trehan for your comments and encouragement. This book is better for your assistance.

I drafted and revised this book during a particularly difficult time in my life, so I must extend a special thanks to my family for supporting me through everything. Neil, you are the epitome of a supportive partner. Emily, I am lucky you are my sister. If we had to go through Mom's illness and death, at least I had you to do it with me. And Jayne, my family by choice, thanks for everything.

My mother isn't here to see the final version of this book. But she was the one who introduced me to musical theater, making this book possible. I'd like to thank her for that, and for so much more. Mom, I'm sure that when I complained through the first act of *Cats*, you didn't think I would write an ode to musical theater. But here I am. I will always treasure those days in the car singing along to *The Producers*.

Much appreciation to all of the writers and composers who make musical theater what it is, especially Stephen Schwartz, Winnie Holzman, and Gregory Maguire. Without Elphaba and Galinda, this would not be the same book.

Finally, a huge thank-you to everyone who read and supported my first two books. You are why I do this. I hope you enjoy this one.